Shadowboxing

Shadowboxing

Rowan Mai

Bergamot Press

CONTENTS ▌

CONTENTS

1

Joyride

It was ten to two in the morning, I had just about closed down Zeke's. I could hear the bartender and waitress laughing, punch-drunk, as they cracked jokes and slung garbage bags into the clanking dumpster out back. Cold air stole in from the metal door they'd propped open. I should have been exhausted after a long week at work, but instead I was drumming my fingers on the bar and thinking about where to go next. I pushed back from the bar, checked I'd left more than enough tip. I called a good night to the staff out back, but didn't wait to see whether they'd heard me.

Out front, I pulled up my coat collar, tipped my head up to breathe the frosty air deeply. It rushed in against the nerves jangling inside me, seemed to only coax them higher. I set out fast. It was three miles home from here, down Charleton until I hit the main drag of Fairway, but I needed the walk, or I was going to get myself into a fight for no reason as soon as I could find the chance.

With who? I laughed at myself softly. Even on a Friday night, the city was quiet, stuck to early hours; Zeke's was one of the only bars that stayed open past midnight.

Charleton was old, winding its way down a steep hillside, cluttered with small businesses built off of spidery alleyways. I strode past them in a rush, one of the scant handful of people still out. Streetlights glinted off of smeary storefront windows and the occasional patches of cobblestoned sidewalk. I went faster and faster, smelling snatches of wood-smoke and garbage curling through the cold air.

Soon I was only one or two turns away from the bottom of the hill. I would have rushed right by the last alleyway if I hadn't heard a clatter, the rustle of shifting bodies, and a distinct gasp, which might have been a choked-off cry.

I checked my headlong progress, pivoted slowly. I took one, two steps into the alley. The sounds of a scuffle were distinct now. Slowly my jittering senses fixed on the dark shapes at the back of the alleyway.

There were three or four men, crouching or bent over. And there was a wheelchair, sitting askew, and there was a slight figure sliding out of it. One of the bent figures had an arm around its neck, one hand on its mouth.

I took a breath.

I am not always conscious of my size. I was conscious of it now as I strode up the alleyway: my height, my breadth, the distance that each stride ate up. I should have said "I'm calling the cops," and let them run—they could have had a knife, a gun—but I didn't. I wanted this.

My dad once told me, "Holding on to anger is like holding on to a hot coal to throw it at someone. You'll only burn yourself." But I had found that the older I got, the better I was at throwing the coal, and making it count.

They scattered as I approached, mostly. One took off right away, one backed off, and only one stayed with his arms around the man in the wheelchair. It didn't take much to scare off the man backing away, hands raised. I just had to take a few more steps, raise my fists, and give him a swift but deliberate look-over. He took off, too, though I kicked him in the back of the knee as he passed, so he fell badly, crying out. I hoped he skinned his hands, jammed a wrist.

"Hey, man, it was just a joke, this guy is my friend here—" said the remaining man, finally lifting his hands off the man in the wheelchair, who was sliding to the ground as I watched.

I wanted to spit. I rushed in, cutting in around the wheelchair, and caught the last man with an open hand to his chest, bulling against him until he slammed into the alley's back wall. His head whipped back against the wall, and he grunted in pain. With my other hand, I grasped his wrists together, digging a nail into the tendons at the base of one wrist to dissuade him from trying anything, and looked him over rapidly. *I could hit you in the face a bunch of times with my fist*, I wanted to tell him. Instead I reached roughly into his pockets until I had found his wallet.

I slapped him in the face with that—a few times, and then a few more. Then, "Get out," I said. "You'll be hearing from the police." *And your friends shouldn't hope I'll forget their faces, either.*

I let go of his wrists. Breathing hard, he edged around me, then pounded off across the pavement. I watched the mouth of the alleyway until the sound of his footfalls faded.

"Holy shit," said the man who was now awkwardly leaning his back against the edge of the seat of his wheelchair. "Thank you."

I stood for a second longer, flexing my hands, looking out at the night. Blood was pounding in my ears.

After another moment, I turned to face him fully.

"Before you ask," he said, "my arm's just like this. They didn't hurt me."

My vision seemed to settle, broaden out from the burning focus that the confrontation had provoked. For the first time, I really looked at the man with the wheelchair.

He was slight, mid-twenties, with big dark eyes, longish dark hair, roughly curling. His legs looked shrunken, crooked. From the awkward way he was holding them, I wondered if he could move them much. And his right arm was shrunken, too, held tightly to his chest, the wrist bent at an unnatural angle. The fingers pointed downward, and were flexing in and out spasmodically. He was starting to shake, but, absurdly, gave me a reassuring smile, as if I was the one who needed it.

Even that shaky smile was lovely.

I put a hand over my mouth, pressing down the hot blood still surging in me. This guy needed me now.

"Okay," I said, rubbing my jaw, "are you sure? How can I help you?"

His name was Asher, he told me as he instructed me how to get him back into his wheelchair. "I'm Roy," I said, my face right next to his as I hugged him under the armpits and carefully lifted. He leaned forward over my shoulder, a warm weight, his one arm gently pressing against my back. He was so light.

Once he was seated, I stood back to let him arrange himself. I watched as he grabbed each half of a seatbelt and buckled himself in, all with his left hand. Whatever condition he had, it looked like that hand was affected, too; he moved it slowly, didn't seem to be able to exert much pressure. Maybe it was just the shock.

"Do you want to find someplace warm? Catch your breath?" I asked, watching him shake.

He used his hand to adjust how his legs were resting, finally looked situated. He moved his hand to the joystick at the end of the armrest. "I think," he said, "I'll be okay once I get home. They barely had a chance to start anything before you arrived and broke up the party. But would you..." He took a deep breath, and I could tell he was hesitating to ask me for more help.

"Would you mind walking me to the bus stop? Otherwise I can call someone."

"I'll walk you," I said automatically. Who knew how long it would take someone else to get here, if he could even get someone to answer the phone? He saw in my face that I meant it, and smiled again, just slightly, but it was enough to send a shiver of feeling through me.

I set my mind on the practical again. "Are you warm enough?"

"Oh, yeah—" he gestured at his short down coat, scarf, and boots, which was much more than I was wearing.

I nodded, turned to the mouth of the alleyway. He pressed on a joystick on the armrest to bring the small wheelchair into motion, and we set off into the night.

2

At the Bus Stop

"Your stop's on Fairway?" I asked as we moved off down Charleton. After a quick glance to confirm the absence of cars in either direction, Asher had abandoned the sidewalk for the street itself; I guessed he wasn't a fan of the stretches of cobblestones. I paced alongside him; his wheelchair could go at a good clip.

"Yeah, the Ridge Street stop," he confirmed, which put us at about a ten-minute walk, and then however long it would take the bus to come. Thanks to taxpayers with an enthusiasm for public transit, buses ran every thirty minutes even this late at night, but that still meant it could take an hour end-to-end for him to get home. He must have been thinking about the same thing, because he said, squinting upward at the sky, "Honestly, I think I could use the air. I need to chill out after that. I don't think I'd be able to settle down if I called a cab and went home right away."

I shrugged, not comfortable making a recommendation either way. At that point we hit Fairway, turned left onto the broad, well-lit expanse. I noted, as he regained the sidewalk, that his shakes had subsided.

We continued in silence for a couple of blocks. I watched my breath puff out ahead of me, glanced around at buzzing streetlights, closed storefronts, dried leaves skittering down the sidewalk, and—not too often, I hoped—Asher next to me. His profile looked tense, and he let loose an occasional hard, audible exhalation. But he looked resolute to me, his mouth set. He wasn't all right, but there were no signs of panic. I felt relieved.

I watched the streetlights move over his hand on the joystick. It was nicely shaped, with long fingers. I could still see the fingers of his bent-down right hand flexing in and out, but slowly now, almost meditatively, instead of the rapid twitches I'd seen before.

"Long week?" Asher said suddenly. It was so banal, out-of-place, that I almost laughed. I might have grinned for a second.

"Huh?"

"You're not much of a talker, is what I meant," he said, turning his face up to me and grinning mischievously. His eyes crinkled at the corners.

I tilted my head to one side and started rubbing one ear, taken aback by his sudden pivot. I tried again to ignore how his smile made me feel. "Mm..."

He continued to grin up at me, raising his eyebrows demonstratively. The headlights of a rare passing car rolled over his face and then off again.

It was my turn to exhale hard now. After that, I sucked my lips in. It felt natural to want to tell him, but that didn't mean I enjoyed doing it. "I used to have a rrrrrrrr... Rrr... *Damn.* Sorry." There it was again, on cue. "I used to have a bad s-s-stutter. It's a lot better now. But it could still be b-better."

Reacting physically, taking the shock and challenge in the alleyway moment by moment, had taken me out of myself. But now I was back in the same old place.

"Ah, shit, sorry, that sucks." Asher was looking ahead again, had lost his grin, and his face was hard to read. But the way he'd said "that sucks" was strangely and immediately comforting, to an extent that belied the casualness of the words. The way he said it seemed to wrap up a lot of things: real acknowledgement, acknowledgement without expecting reassuring qualifications ("but it wasn't really that bad, it made me stronger, God intended this for me"); and a kind of weary acceptance that had to refer to his own state, too. Mostly, I heard companionship.

I went on rubbing my ear without saying anything, until I forced myself to stop fidgeting. It didn't feel right to say "thanks," so I just gave him a nod and hoped he knew what I meant. For the next few minutes, I forced myself to keep looking straight ahead, no stealing glances at him.

We were almost at the bus stop. After a couple cars went by, sending a slight gust of wind and a low flurry of leaves by us, he cleared his throat and said, "I keep thinking, if I were you, I would be *dying* to know how the hell I got myself in that situation in the alley."

I laughed, finally. "Yeah, well."

"It's both a worse and better story than what you're probably hoping for, depending on how you look at it."

"I don't even know what kind of story I'm sssss... s-supposed to hope for."

"I like it—no expectations are even better than low expectations. Well, I'll cut you a deal since you're obviously so eager to pry it out of me." He grinned again, and I felt a pleasant flicker of warmth. "I'll tell you my tale of woe once we get to the bus stop, and if we have time before the bus gets here. Deal?"

"Deal." I *did* want to know, but it wasn't my style to go needling after stuff like that.

He paused his wheelchair, taking his hand off to offer me a handshake. I hesitated, then took it. His hand felt so small. He held on for one second, two seconds longer than would have been expected, his slender fingers pressing gently. I wasn't sure what my face was doing during that time, so when he finally let go, I quickly composed it into an imitation of a businessman —mouth firmed, eyes hooded—and gave him a crisp nod.

He was smiling to himself as we pulled into the bus stop. It wasn't a windy night, but even so, it felt a touch warmer inside the shelter. I found I appreciated it, though I'd been comfortable enough during our brisk walk. I wondered about him; it registered now that his hand had been cold.

(Even so, I felt like I wanted to live in the memory of that handshake.)

It seemed as if he'd had a similar realization, because he was fishing around inside of a coat pocket with his one hand now. "This is going to take me a little while," he said in an undertone, as he drew out a pair of gloves. Then he turned his face up to me and raised his voice to continue, "So I'm going to ask you to work on something else for me."

"Thought I was going to get to hear your story now. I don't see the bus."

"Yeah, but I'm hedging my bets."

I looked at him quizzically.

He swiveled his wheelchair to face me more squarely, leaned back, and put his hand on his knee. "Look, Roy."

The way he said it, my heartbeat was already speeding up with an uncomfortable expectancy.

He continued, "You're very intriguing, you're very handsome, and I like the way you look at me. And you saved me tonight. So I'm going to ask you to do me the favor of putting your number in my phone, right now, so I don't risk getting whisked away into the night without ever seeing you again."

My mouth opened a little. I closed it again, looked away. Then I put my hand out and tried to give him a smile until he handed me his phone. I found that my face was hot.

Fucking relax, I told myself. *You're not fifteen.* I typed my info into his contacts, restrained the nervous urge to toss the phone from hand to hand when I was done.

Meanwhile, Asher had gotten one glove onto his bent right hand, and was now using his teeth to pull the other by the cuff onto his left hand. The way the right glove hung loose made it clear that that hand was significantly smaller.

Finished, he flexed his left hand a few times, then leaned back in his chair and looked up at me, with the slightest smile on his lips. The glare of the bus stop's lighting made his eyes look even larger and darker. I handed his phone back over, and then, struck by a thought, reached into my pocket for the wallet of the man from the alleyway, while gesturing "just one second" to Asher. I flipped it open, looked at his ID—William Riley. (I should have checked that there *was* ID before I let him run, I told myself reproachfully. From experience, I knew that was only the first of many *should-have*'s that would be visiting me that night.)

I flipped the wallet shut again, and extended it to Asher. "Might want this too." He looked blank. "For the police rrrrr... report," I added. After a moment, he registered what I was referring to, and his face instantly clouded over.

"Thanks," he said, and took it reluctantly, unzipping his coat to slide it away into an inside pocket. I felt a pang of regret, as if I had soured the moment, and looked away to the side, pretended I was checking for the bus.

"Okay," Asher said after a pause, "bus schedule says that we have about eight minutes before the next bus is due. Storytime?"

"Sssss..." I paused. "Storytime."

We smiled at each other.

3

Scheherezade

"Once upon a time," Asher said, "on the—what is it? —the seventeenth day of the tenth month of the year, a young man found himself in the happy circumstance of having arranged for himself *a date*. Now, this young man, being a big ol' queermo—" I snorted, and his smile widened "—had resorted to use of the magical rite known as Grindr to find himself said date. He had also, for the very first time, made himself a dating profile—magical, of course—that didn't mention the fact that he was in a wheelchair, because he was sick of not getting any dates.

"It felt like giving up, but also like not that dumb of a move. Also, I *did* use one photo where you could see pretty much the whole situation, so." I had been wondering about that, and pulled my mouth to one side.

Asher sighed, with heat, and thrust his hand through his hair before composing himself again.

"Lo," he continued, gesturing with a flourish, "came the night of the date. The other guy had seemed cute and smart and interestingly employed, and they had exchanged many a humorous missive via the mystical Grindr. Our young man was way excited, got himself dressed up real nice, but not nice enough to look like he was trying too hard, and headed out early for the tavern they had agreed upon for their amorous encounter. This meant he had many, many a minute to find a seat that would sort of but not totally hide the wheelchair, and to freak out over how this guy was going to react when he saw it, the arm, etc."

Asher paused here. Somewhere along the way he had stopped meeting my eyes. I gave him a little while, before deciding that he might appreciate a push. "So?"

He sighed. "The other guy got there just about exactly when the date was supposed to start, which I thought was a good sign. Not so good when he got close enough to see the wheelchair. I've gotten it before, obviously, but I *still* hope I forget what his face looked like. It's just..." He paused again. "We got like five minutes in past 'hey, it's great to meet you in person, how are you doing tonight' before he said, 'Look, sorry, this isn't going to work' and basically left right then. I think he was staring at my hand the whole time, too.

"I don't know if he never even really looked at the one photo, or if he did and told himself that he could deal with it when he came to it, and then *couldn't*..." Asher looked lost.

My gut was churning with a mixture of anger, disgust, and, unexpectedly, fear—the fear that I guessed Asher had felt all that time, waiting in the bar, and the fear that I felt myself, still, anytime I was expected to really talk with anyone I didn't know. "That makes me sick," I said, simply, to Asher. "I'm rrrrrr... really sssss... sss-sorry."

"Thanks," he said, looking up at me. He didn't seem to notice how long it took me to get through three words. His face was serious.

A single pedestrian walked by swiftly on the other side of the street, the first one we'd seen in a while, a woman huddled into a long parka. Asher watched her as he continued. "So I sat there and felt shitty about myself, shitty about him, hoped no one had noticed but was pretty sure that at least a couple people had because I could see so much pity in their faces. God. I went back and forth for a while about whether I should just get the hell out and never show my face there again, but ended up staying. I pretty much never drink because I already don't feel like I'm in control of my body, but I had one drink just to make a point to myself and the world. I made it last for like four hours, and the waitress was really nice to me about it. I had a book with me, at least, so for a while I tried to read, and for a while I just kind of glazed over. Then I realized it was so late that the place was about to close. I headed out and like *one block later* ran into the three shitheads you met.

"The insane thing is, I don't even think they were that drunk, they were just really shitty, dumb people. Or like, one or two of them was super shitty, and the rest were dumb enough to go along with it. The plan, apparently, was to steal my wheelchair for just a *little* bit, do a joyride up and down

Charleton, then plop me back in, pat me on the ass, and send me on my way. I'm still not sure whether that's better or worse than just straight-up deciding to mug a disabled guy.

"And thaaaat's the story of my terrible, horrible, no good, very bad day. Up to the part where you came in." He smiled crookedly at me, then looked down. "I try really, really hard not to go in for self-pity, but god. What can you *say* to all of that?" He looked so tired then, and so bitter, that it aged him, hollowed his face out.

All I could do was hold my hands out wide and shake my head. I hoped my face showed what I was feeling.

And then, on an impulse, I took a step closer to him, and reached out to cup one of my hands against the side of his face.

He closed his eyes, and leaned into the pressure. I loved the warmth of his cheek. The tension around his eyes and mouth eased, until his face looked peaceful. He had long lashes.

I don't know how much later, he said, "I think the bus is coming." He opened his eyes again. I could hear it now, too, the deep surge of the engine. It came into view around the nearest curve of Fairway, sweeping its pale lights ahead of it.

I stepped back, let my hand drop. "Be safe," I said.

"I'll call you," he said. The bus pulled to a stop alongside us.

***

It was almost 3:30 AM by the time I got home; normally I never stayed up past 11. (I had been proud of myself for agreeing to a pretty late-night date tonight; so much for that.) The combination of the night's events and the near-silent bus ride had left me in a kind of glitchy daze, exhausted but raw-feeling. I wondered if I would be able to fall asleep.

I pulled up my wheelchair facing the bathroom mirror as I pulled off gloves, scarf, coat. Phone went between my legs for temporary safekeeping. As I eased my bunched jacket sleeve off my right arm, I caught myself looking myself over in the mirror, in the half-light that reached it from the hallway, trying to see with the eyes of the guy from Grindr—his name had been James. A nice, steady name, I had thought. James' eyes reported not just that I had crippled legs and a crippled arm, which I, Asher, considered factual, but that they were distorted, unwholesome, repellent. My contracted arm was in-sectoid, mantis-like, or maybe like a plucked chicken wing.

My heart was racing again, and my stomach churned. With a twinge, my right arm contracted a bit, and the fingers of that hand fluttered in and out. I always wished I could control them better. (Forget about poker face; give me poker hands.)

Actually it was easier to be mad about James than to think about the three guys in the alley, which was, on some level, possibly why I was sitting and doing this. I sighed, broke eye contact with mirror-Asher, pseudo-James, and rolled all the way into the bathroom, where I splashed water on my face and neck and toweled it off.

In my bedroom, I plugged in my chair to charge overnight, and then transferred to my bed before undressing. Lying back against a couple pillows made it easier for me to get my jeans down over my hips and butt in order to begin the process of extracting my stiff, bent legs. Finally, I flung my clothes across the neighboring dresser. Then I eased myself up until I could pull the comforter back and toss it over my legs, which fell to one side. They would be sore in the morning, I knew, but I was feeling too off to be responsible and reach for a pillow to tuck under them. I used my good arm to push myself further down under the covers, gradually, and then reached out for my phone.

I flopped back against the pillows, unlocked my phone. Roy's contact info was still the first window open; on the bus I hadn't been able to do anything but sit and stare.

"Hi, Roy," I whispered.

I let the phone drop to the side. I'd forgotten to turn off the wall switch as I came in, but there was no way I was doing anything about that now. So I stared up at the glaring ceiling light and thought about Roy.

How the hell did three such insane things happen in one night? Grindr date from hell, attempted-wheelchair-theft gang ("what the fuck," I whispered to myself), capped off by rescue from mysterious silent stranger with a vigilante complex, and also a convenient case of the gays. Roy was so weird and improbable, in fact, that part of my brain had been screaming at me during all of that time with him *not* to trust him, *not* to like him. But I liked him. A lot. I hoped it wasn't just because he obviously had a thing for me, a thing so obvious that even someone with abjectly low self-esteem where romance was concerned could perceive it.

If I didn't trust him entirely, it was because he was honestly a little scary. Not all the time, but when he wasn't actively being scary, he was still pretty weird.

I turned my head on the pillow, thinking furiously. What did I really know about Roy?

So he had, or had had, a serious speech impediment. I couldn't blame him if that had made him weird. I often thought (guiltily, because I had friends with cerebral palsy who were nonverbal or close to it) that I was glad that my CP hadn't also affected my speech because if there's one thing that can make people assume real fast that you're *also* mentally disabled, it's a serious speech impediment.

But it wasn't just his near-silence, his long pauses and looks where other people would feel compelled to express themselves, or at least provide some harmless chatter. His silence had *flavors*. There was some kind of intensity rolling off of him at all times, a kind of heat, and I didn't know how to parse it. That was scary.

And then there had been the fight in the alleyway. Not just the fact that he chose to fight, instead of calling the police, but the fact that he had been obviously *restraining* himself the whole time. I hadn't noticed it at the time—I was too busy trying to breathe and not surrender to the wall of panic that wanted to press me flat, I had *never* felt so vulnerable before, never never never. But moments of the fight had suddenly returned to me with unnerving clarity as we headed down Charleton. The moment when his still silhouette at the mouth of the alleyway suddenly broke into a sprint, pounding down the alley toward us, the brutal ease with which he landed blows on the fleeing men, the way that he hunched back into himself like an animal before he rushed to pin the last man, the instigator, against the alley wall. After that, they were behind me, I was *falling out of my chair*—but I heard some of the brief scuffle that ensued, the man's whimpering breath, the dull slaps that I realized much later were Roy hitting him with his own wallet. The wallet that still rested in the inside pocket of my coat. I hadn't wanted to touch it, look at it again.

I guess I should have been flattered that this stranger wanted that badly to fuck up the gang of three. But a small part of what had shaken me in that alleyway was the sense that his anger was... impersonal, that this was a freak incident that happened to tap into a well of anger that went deep, was always there.

I wasn't used to being close to anger, let alone that much of it.

It didn't help that Roy was *huge*. I was bad at guessing heights, which was easy to blame on my vantage point, but he was definitely over six foot, and built like a locomotive. A locomotive with huge hands. I am, of necessity, a coward when it comes to anything physical, and—I didn't know where I was going with this, Roy hadn't offered *me* the slightest hint of violence. But he looked like he was designed to walk through brick walls.

I shook my head. Chewing everything over, overanalyzing as I liked to, was a better alternative to lying in bed paralyzed with fear, but it wasn't helping me sleep. Did I even want to sleep? There was something comforting about the idea of being awake to see the sun come up. Thank god tomorrow was Saturday.

What else did I know about Roy? He was pretty bad at not showing his feelings. I pressed my face further into my pillow and smiled to myself. I wanted to think about the fun stuff now.

I had really liked the way he looked me over, the first time he really looked at me. At first it had been neutral, methodical, ready to assess the damage—not horrified, not full of pity. That neutrality alone had been enough to help me start calming down. *Okay*, his look said, *what next?* (*See*, said a voice in my brain now, *not angry all the time.*)

And then, as he looked at me for longer, something warmer broke through. He had a square jaw, a mouth that he tended to hold tightly, eyes with tension lines at the corners, straightish middling brown hair cut short—traits that all went along with his quasi-military intensity. (Had he been in the military?) But somehow they went *soft* as he looked me that first time.

And I saw it happen again and again, during that hour or however long we spent together. If we weren't really talking, or if we were talking about something that made him angry (like the story of my shitty night), the tension would gather up again in his brows and the set of his jaw. But if he really looked at me, it just... dissolved. He looked soft. There was no other way to put it.

It made me feel really good. So did the way he kept looking at me while trying to make it look like he wasn't looking at me, and *not* in the way I always got from strangers. He just looked... like he was enjoying it. Like he wanted more.

Also, I liked his voice, what little I had heard of it. Deep, with a little bit of gravel to it, it seemed to emanate from behind his sternum. It felt like a presence instead of a voice.

I realized that the cheek I was lying against was the cheek he had held his hand against. His hand had been chilled, so it had sent an extra thrill through me. I thought about the largeness and firmness of that hand, its comfortingly rough texture, the simple shock of contact, of *presence* (that word again). I didn't know if anyone had ever touched me that way before. I'd gotten as far as kissing a few guys before, a little bit of messing around, but it had all been really shy, kind of stilted. Nothing with that immediacy of emotion. The naked expression of tenderness.

I flung my arm over my eyes, overwhelmed. Then I reached out for my phone, flipped open Roy's contact info again. I hit the text button and propped the phone in the crook of my bad arm so I'd have something to type against.

"Hi," I typed. "This is Asher. I got home safely, and I hope you did too. Thank you again for everything." I hit *send*, and then typed, "Would you like to get coffee on Sunday?"

I hovered my thumb over *send*. Was Sunday too soon? Would it come off as desperate? *Damn the torpedoes,* I thought, deliriously. I hit *send*.

4

View from the Morning

Of course I ended up falling asleep right before the sunrise; so much for that romantic notion. Luckily, somewhere along the way I had ended up having the sense to tuck a pillow under my knees, so I didn't completely hate myself in the morning. Still, my back and neck were killing me when I woke up, not to mention my wrist; it had to be from the stress of last night. It was also 11 A.M., later than I could remember waking up in at least a year. Outside, the sun was shining weakly through an even, milky haze of cloud, which was about how I felt.

I swore to myself for a while before I even tried getting up, just feeling the sharp twangs of pain as I shifted my back and arms minutely. Finally I got myself up onto my one elbow and levered up from there to a sitting position, wincing the whole time. The only good thing that I could immediately see was the fact that I had gone to bed in nothing but boxers, which meant there was very little between me and a scalding-hot shower.

One literally painfully slow transfer later, I rolled into the bathroom. I felt scummy, disoriented. I set the shower tap to hot and let it run for a good few minutes before I began my transfer onto the shower seat. Then I let the water pound at me for a while, with my eyes closed. Slowly I started to massage my right hand and wrist; I gasped the first time that I gently flexed the hand back, felt the good-bad hurt of working against the tension in the contracted joint. I would never have anything resembling function in that arm, but regular stretching would at least prevent the contracture from progressing, which, in theory, meant that my arm would never have to feel any damn worse than it did right now.

Fifteen minutes later, I had toweled off and was back in my chair. I felt markedly better, but still defeated by the idea of trying to be any more functional. For a few minutes I squinted at the blue-white sky. Jagged impressions and sensations tumbled incoherently through my head. Then I went back to bed.

When I woke up again, it was 2 P.M., and I had been having a nightmare about the men in the alley. My heart pounded, and I could feel my sweat soaking into the sheets. I pushed back the comforter and lay there, staring at the ceiling. I'd still forgotten to turn off the overhead light. I wasn't used to sleeping in the middle of the day, so I felt even more unhinged.

Grasping for a sense of orientation, I reached for my phone. My heart skipped again when I saw that there was an unread text. From Roy.

I had, to my amazement, completely forgotten about Roy. For a while, it seemed, there had been nothing but the three men and me in the alley.

I thumbed the message open. "Thanks for letting me know you got home safely," was all it said.

I let the phone drop. I stared at the ceiling for a minute longer, refusing to feel anything. Then I levered myself up again. "I refuse to let my weekend feel any shittier," I said out loud. My heart was still hammering, and my mouth was dry.

I transferred once again, rolled out to the living area. I turned on music, whatever had already been queued in my playlist. I drank a whole glass of water, then another, and then did my best to keep working out the tension in my back, stretching my arm overhead, doing twists, swearing some more, leaning forward to lie over my knees as much as I could without crunching up my right arm. When my back was beginning to feel looser, smoother, the little red-hot flares of pain less frequent, I transitioned into doing the core conditioning exercises I tried to keep up with daily; working out my abs was supposed to help stabilize the back tension that came from my overall crookedness. This pain was more manageable, almost a welcome distraction. My legs even did me the courtesy of not going into spasm.

By the end of it, my heart felt like it was running fast only in a good, exercised kind of way; I could feel renewed circulation tingling through my legs and toes. Cleaning up, getting dressed, and making and eating lunch occupied another hour or so. After, I pulled a random book off the shelf—it turned out to be a collection of architectural sketches—and sat with it in my lap for another I-don't-know-how-long, just paging through it, pausing where I wanted to look at something, and sometimes just because I was staring at nothing, trying not to think about the alleyway.

Eventually, though, I realized that I was actually looking at the pictures, that my attention had settled enough for me to kind of drift among the rafters and gables, finding pleasing patterns and shapes more so than structures. And that felt really nice.

Still. "I just wanted to have something to look forward to," I said out loud, pathetically, as I rolled back to my bedroom, where my phone was still on the nightstand.

I turned on the screen, and there was an unread message from Roy. I was ashamed to feel one of my legs kick up and start spasming in response; it had been waiting for this, I thought spitefully.

The message read, "I would love to get coffee on Sunday. Where and when would be good?"

I let my head drop, and closed my eyes. When I looked up again, I could see a narrow slice of the sun sliding out from behind a screen of shredded clouds. "We did it!" I informed it.

***

"I'll be honest," Asher was saying, "I got a little nervous when you didn't text back for a while. Phones turn us all into teenage girls."

"I was afraid it might feel that way," I admitted. "Thhh... that's why I checked."

Asher gave me a brilliant smile in return. I felt undeserving. "I'm just... not used to the dating thing," I continued. I wrapped my hands around my coffee mug and watched his face.

He'd picked a spacious café near the Ridge St. stop. It was late on Sunday afternoon. Asher looked tired, but the sunlight flooding in the windows made his skin glow and put golden lights in his warm brown eyes. He'd ordered a tea, and was absent-mindedly leaning forward to hold his right hand, the small one, over the steam from it.

"You're a lot b-braver than I am," I added. It was a thought that had been on my mind a lot since Friday night.

His smile had widened even further. When it was clear I wasn't going to say anything else, he said, "I hope this doesn't make you self-conscious, but I think that might be the most things you've said to me in a row so far, and I'm feeling good about that. I feel like that's a good start to a date—which I feel like I can say because you said 'dating,' so thanks for that also." He paused, and the way he smiled made me think he might be nervous that he was talking too much. "But I'm interested," he went on, "in this idea of 'braver than me,' considering that you're the one who, you know, was ready to beat up three guys on a stranger's behalf."

"That's different," I said. "I wwww... would have done that aaa... a-anyway."

He looked puzzled, and I didn't feel like I could explain without messing up more. I didn't feel as nervous as I had expected to—seeing his face again had put me at ease in a way that I couldn't explain to myself—but my stammer was still acting up for some reason. I could feel the pressure building in my chest.

He must have understood my frustrated look, because he paused to make sure I wasn't going to continue, and then said, "Do you mean something like—it wouldn't have occurred to you to do anything else in that situation?"

"Yes," I managed.

"Hm. There is that classic question: does bravery mean not feeling fear, or does it mean feeling fear but choosing to go ahead anyway? Or hackneyed question, whatever."

I shrugged, raised my eyebrows.

"Well. If it makes you feel better, when it comes to stuff like asking you out—I just go with it, if it feels really right. So I guess that's kind of like you rushing into a fight. But I get terrified afterwards." He took a sip of his tea. "I think, for me, talking is an easy way to... engage with the moment, if that makes sense. I guess it's been my only reliable way of being like, 'Hey, I'm a person! Listen to me!'" He paused for another sip. "I hope—I hope if we keep spending time together you'll tell me, or show me, if it feels like I'm talking *over* you. Or not listening to you."

I didn't know what else to do but reach out and hold my hand over his, where it was still resting against his mug of tea. He actually blushed. The café suddenly felt far too crowded, even though there was only a handful of other people around, scattered among mostly empty tables.

"Um," he said. "I guess this is normally where I should ask you to tell me more about you, but I don't know how you're feeling about that."

"I cuhhh... cuh... I'll try," I said, without moving my hand. "Um, I work for a landscaping business. Building, planting. A lot of moving ssss... stuff on and off of trucks. It mmm... mm... it *means* I listen to what people want done, what they're excited about, and do it. And I get to work with plants a lot."

"What's your favorite plant?"

"Trees," I said instantly. "Esss-ss... esp... particularly conifers. Cypresses are great. And redwoods, but I've n-n-never gotten to see a really big one." The smile playing on his lips as he listened was enchanting. I felt as if I could see a forest growing behind his eyes, dense, green, inviting.

"Those grow on the west coast, right? You haven't gotten to go out there yet?"

"Ssss... Seattle once, but not California, where the national park is. My sssss... sis-sister lived in Seattle for a while." I was relieved to have gotten the second "Seattle" out without a hitch.

"Big sister or little? Are you close?"

I paused for a while, marshalling my words, and trying to relax my jaw—always a losing battle, it seemed—to keep the stuttering at bay. I had thought a lot about what I was going to say next, but never actually had a reason to tell anyone before. "Little. And, my fffff... f-family, I feel like we're all different ssss... s-species. We r-respect each other, but we don't get each other. I g-guess it's good that we're all independent, nothing to worry about. But my sister... I sometimes wish I knew how to be c-closer. Visiting her in Ssss... S-Seattle was one of the only things we've actually done together as adults."

"What 'species' is she? What do you think it would be like to be closer with her?"

And so on, until I'd ended up talking more than I usually did in a month, and the sun was starting to set. I wasn't even fully aware of what I was saying, after a while, except when my stammer got really stuck and I had to think about rephrasing, which happened less and less. I was just watching his smile, the lights in his eyes, and how much he, bafflingly, seemed to enjoy listening to me.

Until—"Hey," he said, "would you like a change of scene?"

We had both finally finished our drinks, and from the light, the sun would have been right around the horizon. "Sure?" I said, unsure of what he was thinking. But it was true that walking would have felt nice at that point. I wondered what it was like to not be able to stand up, shake yourself out, get your blood moving. Asher had been stretching his back out a lot, with his one arm extended or bent overhead, and occasionally used his hand to shift his legs to one side or the other, which I guessed might help a little. I'd noticed, too, that his legs sometimes seemed to move by themselves, kicking up from the hip stiffly or trembling suddenly; it didn't seem like he could control them.

"I was just thinking," Asher said, "it might be nice to be somewhere a bit more private. If that sounds nice to you, too, we could grab the bus over to my place, and I could cook you dinner. What do you think?"

"I would love that," I said.

5

Different Species

On the bus ride over, I learned that Asher was 26—four years younger than me. (That was how much he'd been forcing—no, coaxing—me to talk about myself at the café, that I hadn't learned even his age till then.) He was an only child, and hadn't moved out from his parents' until just last year, but not for lack of encouragement. He was close with his parents, not just out of necessity, and they'd always pushed him to be independent. But it had taken him longer to finish college, and after that, it had still taken him a few more years to feel ready to leave home. Once he did, his parents had helped him find an apartment—one that was closer to his job than his parents' place, and accessible.

He worked as a data scientist, crunching spreadsheets—healthcare info, all the paperwork from doctors' offices. He waved off further explanation, said that he was in it mainly for the job security. "I don't mind admitting that I care more about good medical insurance right now than being excited about my job. It would be nice to find something I care more about, but I'm happy to work with nice people, doing something that feels, eh, moderately useful."

I smiled. I was savoring the process of building out a picture of Asher's daily life, his family, how he thought about things. It was clear that he was more of a thinker than me—or more of an intellectual. (After all, I spent most of my time thinking to myself, even if I hadn't bothered finishing college.) He read a lot, for example, which I didn't always have patience for, and especially about art, which had always intimidated me. But it struck me that even when he went somewhere in conversation I couldn't quite follow, I liked the nimbleness and excitement with which he thought and spoke, the way he could sort of dance back and forth across a topic, come at it from different angles. I could almost see his thoughts moving over his face like a flickering light.

"Hey, one thing," Asher was saying then, with a slight change of tone. I brought my attention back to center, looked at him questioningly. "Kind of a change of topic. I get the sense that it's not your thing to ask about personal details, but I think it would make me feel more comfortable if I could tell you a bit about my disability. So you know what you're getting into, I guess. Is that okay with you?" It all came out in a rush, and he sucked his lips in nervously at the end, the first time I had seen him do that.

I nodded, widening my eyes to show my seriousness.

"Do you know what my disability is? Just checking."

I shook my head. I hadn't been sure if there was something wrong with his bones, or his muscles, or maybe both.

He spoke very softly, so that his voice almost blended with the muffled roar of the bus engine, but more slowly this time. "Okay, I have something called cerebral palsy—CP for short. It happened when I was a baby, because I got stuck coming out for like twenty minutes, which meant I was deprived of oxygen. That hurt the part of my brain that controls my muscles. There are a bunch of different effects that can have, but I have the kind of CP that makes your muscles really tight. Sometimes they go into spasm. So if you see me start to shake, that's what's going on. It's not serious, but it can be really uncomfortable."

He was searching my face the whole time he was telling me this, anxiously watching. Without being able to help himself, he was waiting for rejection again.

"Thank you for telling me," I said. Fixed in my brain was the image of a tiny blue infant, with wisps of dark hair, gasping for breath. I cleared my head, looked at the Asher in front of me now, with tousled hair and lips slightly parted in anxious expectation. I reached out to his nearest hand, which was the right one, the small one. I held his fingers gently, barely applying pressure, just making enough contact to feel his warmth, the softness of his skin. "Just—let me know whenever there's something I can do to help you out. Or if there's sss-something else I should know. Okay?"

The delicate fingertips pressed against mine. "Okay," he said, smiling just a little hesitantly.

***

On the way out, there was some trouble with the bus's wheelchair lift not extending properly for a few minutes. Asher had to roll back into the bus while the driver, a wiry black man in his fifties with a round 'fro, made exasperated noises and jimmied the controls. I was unexpectedly impressed, and grateful, when the other passengers on the bus restrained themselves from staring or making a show of impatience. Though there were a few curious glances, mostly they busied themselves with their phones or books, or stared out the windows at the street, lined with neat, modern, red-brick apartment complexes on one side and small, slightly run-down Victorian houses on the other. I did my best not to loom impatiently over the driver, focused on examining the lift mechanism instead. Luckily the failure wasn't mechanical, it was just on the control end.

Finally the driver could let Asher down, accompanied by many apologies. "Never happened on my watch before, sorry again—you have a nice night now."

"No worries, sorry for holding up the bus," Asher replied, overly generously I thought. We headed out into the twilight.

He had a ground-floor apartment in one of the modern complexes. The front entrance led straight in, no steps up or down, something Asher had mentioned to me when describing his apartment search with his parents earlier. We came in through the kitchen, which opened directly onto the living room; Asher flipped on the lights.

Standing just inside the doorway with my hands in my coat pockets, I looked around. The apartment was sparse, open, and mostly white, with laminate floors, no carpeting. All of the furniture was low, even the kitchen counters. The upper shelves of the rare taller pieces were occupied with a few decorative objects—nothing functional. Books, kitchen supplies, all of that was available at what was waist height on me. The kitchen table was round and had only three chairs pulled up to it; the matching fourth stood in a corner of the living room, next to—I noted with approval—a couple of large potted trees, a weeping fig and a frondy Norfolk Island pine. On the walls there were framed pictures—abstract paintings, or things that looked abstract to me, in colors that I thought of as dark-bright.

"So that's the kitchen and living room, obviously," Asher was saying, "apart from that there's just the bathroom and bedroom, over to the left. The floorplan worked out really well, didn't have to have doorframes widened or such. We did have to have some carpeting ripped out because I wasn't keen on having my 'shoes'—" he pointed down at his wheels "—leave tracks everywhere, and neither was the landlord."

I nodded slowly, still glancing around with interest, piecing together how Asher used the space. All of the furniture, for example, was spaced so his wheelchair could navigate around it —the coffee table wasn't pulled right up to the couch the way most people would have it.

Asher continued, "Tune in next week for another riveting episode of Disability Life Logistics. For now—you can leave your coat and stuff on this coatrack. Shoes can be on or off, I don't mind either way." He was carefully pulling the glove off of his small hand as he spoke, and then unwound his scarf. I was standing just behind him, so it gave me a good look at his long neck, with dark curls clustering just above it. Without thinking about it, I used one hand to start opening my coat, and ran the other along the back of his neck.

He *hissed*. Alarmed, I instantly drew my hand back.

"Oh, no, it's okay," he said hurriedly. "It's just that my back and neck are kind of messed up today. That felt—alarmingly good."

I couldn't resist. Being around him made me *crazy*. His smooth, translucent, golden-pale skin, his smile, the way his dark eyes lit up when he was curious or excited. Half of that weekend, I'd been aching with desire, even just thinking about him on Saturday. I moved both hands to the back of his neck, ran them up and down the sides—he moaned and hunched forward in his chair—then slowly dug in, started gently massaging his neck, the muscles at the tops of his shoulders, and then down to what I could reach of his shoulder blades. He was so small under my hands; it felt so easy to grip him, knead against the fine bones. Even through his coat and sweater, I could feel that he had almost no fat, just taut muscle and bone.

He was starting to collapse over his knees, sighing. His left arm hung over the front of his seat. I tried not to put any of my real weight onto him, not wanting to press on his drawn-up right arm, trapped between his chest and knees; I didn't know if he could move it enough to get it all the way to one side.

That and the fact that he was still in his chair meant I couldn't really get at his lower back.

Still, listening to him sigh, and moan, the warmth of his back, all of it was killing me.

Finally—it was probably only a minute later, but a long minute—I had the presence of mind to stop, place my hands squarely against his shoulder blades for one last press, then gently draw him back up to a sitting position.

He tipped his face up to me, but his eyes were still closed. His lashes trembled as he said, "That was amazing."

I wasn't sure what to say. Despite his apparent contentment, I was suddenly regretful, nervous that I'd gone too far or too fast.

His eyes stayed closed for another few seconds, while he slowly tipped his head from side to side, testing his neck. I used the time to adjust my jeans. When he opened his eyes again, I was still guiltily shifting my stance, and prayed that he didn't notice. All he said was, "What did I do to deserve you?"

***

We had made and finished dinner—pasta with chicken and vegetables—before I felt comfortable asking, "Asher, did you make a police rrrrr... report y-yet?" I'd waited for a lull in the conversation; we were sitting face to face across the table from each other, and the general mood had been a kind of lazy contentment, the conversation pleasantly slow, mostly him talking and me listening, the way I preferred it.

Asher's face went blank, and his gaze immediately dropped. He moved his hand slowly from the tabletop to his lap. "I didn't," he admitted. I had guessed as much from the conspicuous absence of any mention of it. If he had gone forward with anything, I'd have expected to hear by now that I might be called in as a witness.

I reached out and took his hand under the table, but he didn't look at me. I could feel one of his legs starting to tense and bounce.

When he still hadn't said anything, I said, "Look, I d-don't love authority—" he smirked automatically, and I rolled my eyes, realizing what that sounded like coming from a guy who looked and acted like me, "—but those people did a terrible thing. You nnn-n-need to hold them accountable."

Still he didn't meet my eyes. The fingers of his right hand were starting to twitch now, and his mouth was tense. I pressed the hand that I held gently. "Hey," I said.

"Hey," he said, finally. "Thank you." He slid his hand away from mine, and leaned back in his chair, pressing his hand against the side of his face now. "I know it's really irresponsible, but I just—I really don't like thinking about that night."

With my eyes, I invited him to keep talking. The fingers of his right hand flickered in and out.

"It's been pretty bad. I have nightmares about it all night. It feels like... something sick, that I wish I could just put away and wall off from the rest of me." He paused. "And the other part is, I'm afraid to tell my parents. I feel like it'll kill them, to know that this happened to me. If I already can't deal with it myself, I feel like... I can't deal with knowing that other people, my parents of all people, are worrying about it, losing sleep over it..."

And, I guessed, it felt like a failure of his efforts to live independently. But we could talk about that later.

I sat back, thinking through what I'd learned about his relationship with his parents. There was no way I could make recommendations based on what I would have done in the same situation.

"A few thoughts," I said finally. "One, you don't have to d-d-do it alone. I can help you wr-write the rrrrr... report." I mimed myself scribbling frantically first, then pointed to him, and mimed him looking on with skeptical scrutiny, like a fussy client. He smiled in spite of himself. "Two, the l-longer you take to tell your parents, the worse it will feel. Choose a moment that feels rrr-right to you, but *decide* you're going to do it. And if you involve them earlier, they can h-h-help you, too.

"You don't have to do it alone," I repeated, for emphasis.

He was running his hand through his hair now. He looked less pale, though still uncomfortable. "I guess the thing is... I wish I *could* do it alone. But..." His right arm and hand were spasming outright now, jerking back and forth across his chest.

"I get it," I said after another moment, when he seemed unlikely to finish the sentence.

He looked at me full on. "Okay. Thank you. We'll do it—together—in the morning."

6

Lion

It took me a while to realize that the way Asher had said "we'll do it in the morning" implied, even assumed, that I was going to stay over the night. We had just about finished cleaning up after dinner, so it would have been a natural point for me to start saying good night. Uncertain, I turned to him, working out what to say next.

"Asher, w-were you interested... in me staying over?"

He finished racking the last bowl in the dishwasher, and turned his wheelchair to face me. "Oh, geez, yeah. I didn't mean to be so presumptuous." He must have been thinking about what he'd said, too. "Um..." He looked down and started rubbing his hand through his dark curls again. He looked *so* cute. I felt bad for enjoying it, his clear flusterment, but I couldn't not, at least not when it was relatively harmless like this. Finally he said, "I really didn't mean to make assumptions about your... interest. But I would really enjoy it if you stayed over, although I don't know if I want to... do anything." He looked up at me, gauging my reaction.

Again, I wasn't sure if he'd caught me looking him over. I said, "I would love to stay over, too." His eyes lit up. "And we don't have to 'do anything,'" I affirmed quickly. But because he clearly wanted me to, was tense with expectation in that moment, I took two steps forward, leaned down, and kissed him on the lips.

It was a good kiss.

After, I stayed leaning lightly on his armrests for another moment. Asher was flushing delicately, and his eyes, alive with joy, searched my face. "But more of that would be great," he said.

We shared a smile, as if we held a secret between us. Then we kissed again.

***

While Roy was in the bathroom, I grabbed my cellphone and texted Amy. She was one of my closest and oldest friends, and also lived only three blocks away.

I had first texted her that day— "Amy!"—when Roy and I had been about to leave the café, while he had been, again, conveniently in the bathroom.

"Asher!" she'd responded almost instantly; she must have been looking at her phone.

"This is a Responsible Check-In," I had texted, feeling giddy; my fingers felt a little shaky. "I'm about to bring a guy back to my place. I don't know him that well but I like him a lot."

"!!!" she texted back. "ASHER!!!!!!!!"

"I don't feel concerned. But just in case can I call you if anything starts feeling weird?"

"OBVIOUSLY. Thanks for being responsible, chiquito. But ohmahgawd, WHO IS THE GUY? Tell all."

"His name is Roy..." I texted back. I was being coy, but also genuinely bashful.

She texted back a garbled keysmash of excitement, and then "More!!!" At that point Roy came out, so I just typed "More later, bus now," and hastily pocketed my phone.

Over the course of the evening, I'd slipped her updates during down moments—not quite the juicy details she was looking for, but enough both to assure her that everything was going fine, and to let me start testing out what I knew about Roy, and how we seemed to do together, against someone else's instincts. I could count on Amy to be both protective and wildly supportive in the right measure, so seeing her reactions, either skeptical or "go get 'em," helped me feel more secure in my own read of the situation—which was that I liked Roy *a lot*, we had improbably good chemistry, and he hadn't done anything that made me feel unsafe, in fact the opposite.

But he was still weirdly hard for me to read. Even though he was terrible at hiding his emotions, so that watching his face sometimes felt like watching a movie, just with the sound off, and even though he had started talking more and more (a thrilled flutter went through my stomach when I thought about the low gravel of his voice)—I still felt like I couldn't wrap my head around everything that was going on under his quietness and intensity. *You've only known him for less than a day*, I reminded myself.

Now, I pulled up my texts with Amy again, laid my phone on the kitchen table to type into it. "We finished dinner," I sent.

She responded within a minute. "And???"

"I asked him to stay over. Not in a sexy way though."

"OooOOOOOOOOOOoooh I'm still gonna die. You're sure you asked him tho? No pressure?"

"No pressure," I confirmed. "I asked him. And he doesn't make me feel rushed or you know seem to have 'expectations.'" Even typing "expectations" made me flush, pathetically. I continued, "Thanks for listening Amy. It means a lot to me."

"Babe I'm here for you. Also this is so much better than TV." I snorted. "Just pay attention to ANYTHING that makes you feel unsafe. Take it seriously! k?"

"Yes! Thank you," I responded. And then, after thinking it about it for a little while, I typed, "We kissed..."

She sent back another keysmash, even longer this time, and then, "How was it?!"

I couldn't bring myself to crack open Roy's privacy—I highly doubted, for example, that he was in the bathroom frantically texting one of *his* friends about how our kisses had felt. So I answered, "Maybe I'll tell you in person. Gotta keep you on the hook. I go now. Thanks again Gams, you're the best."

"xoxoxo, be wise," she sent.

I smiled down at my phone, then stashed it between my legs and began the moderately tricky operation of pulling off my shirt one-handed—left sleeve off first, with the help of teeth applied to cuff, then over the head, and finally the attack on the right sleeve.

I was just about done extricating myself when Roy emerged from the bathroom, holding his folded clothes in one hand, and wearing just a white undershirt and plaid boxers. He saw my gaze and immediately said, sounding guilty, "I would have asked you for sssss—ssss—sss... *sweatpants*, but—wasn't sure anything would fit."

His stutter on the "s" in "sweatpants" (I'd noticed that he seemed to do the worst with S's and R's) was the toughest it had been all night, I thought. Getting himself out of it, he seemed to have to rock himself backwards, even closed his eyes and shook his head a little, as if trying to reset the system. I felt a pang of sympathy and concern, but was also extremely, undeniably distracted by his body.

"Wow," I said, unable to stop myself. Roy looked great in clothes, with his broad shoulders and chest, square hands, long legs, but without—he looked like a *rock*. He had the kind of dense, allover muscle that made me think of rugby players, guys who really used their whole bodies. (*Unlike me*, said a devastatingly unhelpful voice in my head. My legs jerked upward; I willed myself to ignore it as they slowly relaxed down again, one more slowly than the other.)

I'd noted before that he was tanned a light brown; I could now see that his arms and face were sunned much darker than the rest of him. His arms and legs were also pretty well covered with fine, curling hair that glinted slightly blonder than his head-hair.

"Roy," I said—again I couldn't help it, even though he was getting visibly embarrassed, "I have to ask. Were you in the army or something? What do you *do* to look like that? Is it just your job?"

He was shifting from foot to foot, eyes sliding off to the side. "Job helps, definitely. Wouldn't be happy not doing physical sssss... sstuff. And I did think about Marines, but I used to h-have asthma. Just as a kid, but they're assholes about that. A-anyway, a llll... lot of it now is that I box."

"Box...? *Oh*—boxing!" I leaned back in my chair in surprise.

He looked at me with concern, or maybe wariness. "What?"

"I—I don't know," I admitted, "it totally makes sense, but for some reason I wouldn't have guessed. Boxing, huh. I find that very charming for some reason."

"Charming?" His brow was furrowed.

"It just seems kind of old-fashioned, like midcentury. Like, black-and-white photos of prizefighters." I leaned forward and propped my chin on my hand, smiling at him. "I guess why I like it is, it seems to go with how—old-fashioned I find you. In a nice way."

"Old-fashioned?" His brow was still furrowed, but at least he didn't seem self-conscious anymore, just deeply puzzled.

I laughed, at myself. "I don't know, you're kind of... courtly, I guess I would say. Don't forget, you rescued me. And, I don't know, the way you wait to see how I do things before you see if I need help with stuff like the dishes, but you're always ready to help. The way you watch me without staring—this is all self-centered stuff, sorry. But it's all things that matter a lot, to me. So, thanks."

He reflexively nodded a "you're welcome," without looking convinced. He had even folded his arms, and was leaning forward onto the balls of his feet, as if leaning into his confusion; his face was almost comically *thinky*.

I smiled to myself and moved my wheelchair off into the bedroom. It was only slightly after ten at that point; I had already warned Roy once that I kept early hours. It was important for me to stick to a regular schedule because it significantly cut down on the chances of my having a bad spasm day. (Another reason that Friday night/Saturday morning's hijinks had been so delightful for me.) His perpetual, restless energy made it easy for me to guess that he wasn't a stranger to two or four in the morning, even though his work, he'd mentioned, often required early hours of planning and loading. Even still, he'd made it clear that he was interested in going to bed *with* me (just not that way, yet).

My heart started speeding up as I pulled up alongside the bed, and bent down to grab my transfer board from where I kept it slotted between nightstand and bed. I was already so nervous, and excited, about the idea of someone else being in bed with me, that I suddenly doubted my ability to even sleep.

See it through, soldier, I said to myself. I looked over my shoulder at Roy, who had appeared in the doorway, only marginally less thinky-faced, and then willed myself to focus on the transfer, swiveling my chair to face the foot of my bed. I flipped up my left armrest, and carefully started sliding the smooth plastic board under my rear, so that it provided a continuous surface between me and the bed. As I began scooting one-armed across the board and onto the bed, Roy watched me with that neutral interest that I found immensely soothing —not gaping, just looking to understand how I did things. He even gave a small nod of second-hand satisfaction when I completed the transfer and slid the board out and back next to the nightstand. I let out a breath, pushed my hair back, and smiled up at him. "Would you mind getting the lights?"

He reached out and flicked them off. "Thanks," I said. I had been feeling self-conscious about the next step, so only then, in the dark, did I lie back and start the struggle to remove my jeans. Vanity and I had a confused relationship: I took pride in taking care of my appearance, knew that it gave me a better chance of being taken seriously at first glance. But it also made it harder for me not to carry with me an awareness that certain parts of me—like my shrunken, knock-kneed legs and bent feet—were objectively not attractive. As usual, I deliberately pushed the thought away and focused on the physical task.

I sat up again to manipulate my jeans down over my stiff ankles and feet, and then glanced up as Roy's dark shape moved across the room to peer out through the drawn blinds across the window on the far side of the bed. There wasn't much of a view, just a shallow parking lot fringed with young trees, but when I looked up again, jeans finally off, he was still staring out, a slash of light across his eyes from the slit in the blinds he'd opened.

I pillowed my knees and then wasn't sure what to do next, so I lay back, staring at the ceiling, rubbing the edge of the comforter between thumb and forefinger. My heart sounded, and felt, like a drum section.

I felt the other side of the bed depress. Roy let out a long sigh in the darkness, and then suddenly his warmth and mass pressed all along my side. He reached a heavy arm out across my waist, pulling it gently snug against my other side, tucked his face against my shoulder, snuck his knees under the edge of mine, nudging the pillow slightly out of the way. His breath blew out against my neck as he sighed again, even more deeply.

"This okay?" he said. He already sounded sleepy, to my surprise. During all the other time we'd spent together, he just seemed constantly on alert, keyed-up even when he was clearly enjoying himself.

I had tensed at first, sending pangs through my back, hips, wrist, the works, but now had the sensation that I was slowly melting. Waves of delicious heat were rolling off of his body. His arm across me was so heavy that it felt like a blanket. "Yeah," I said.

"You feel great," he said. His voice rumbled through my chest, a lion-sized purr. "Tell me if I get too much."

"Will do."

"G'night."

"Good night, Roy." He pressed his face closer to my neck, and I moved my hand up to stroke his cheek, running it across the slight rasp of stubble. I closed my eyes. I felt like an insufficient vessel for the happiness rising up in me.

7

Amy Opines

The next morning, when we'd finished filling out the on-line crime report form—an awkward, mostly silent process, where I'd type in short bursts, then trail off, feeling queasy and slightly surreal, until Roy would gesture for me to swivel the laptop keyboard back over to him—I felt a sudden jolt of superstitious fear. Everything that had happened since I'd met Roy had been so improbably *good* that I had the sudden conviction that signing off on the report would bring it all to a close, seal off the freak outgrowth of space-time that had allowed us to briefly coexist.

(The back of my mind also observed, helpfully, that I was probably using this imagined crisis as a distraction from attempting to put a hand on the reality of the men in the alley-way. A memory came back: laughter, as one of them tripped over one of my wheels in passing. I felt the rough impact as he caught his weight on my armrest. I cringed away from his swaying shape. I pushed the memory away.)

As Roy and I kissed good-bye at the threshold of my front door, the question *is this the last time* formed itself clearly in my head, sent a chilly wave of unease through me. My back contracted uncomfortably, tilting me back and to the right. I couldn't look Roy in the eye, either. I think he noticed, too, because a look of puzzled concern crossed his face as he stood up. He said nothing, though. After he'd headed off down the sidewalk, with his rolling, ground-eating gait, I cursed myself bitterly for wasting the moment.

But it wasn't the last time. Over the next couple of weeks, we met up two, three, four more times—sometimes in the city, sometimes at my place. Every time, I still couldn't quite believe that he was real, that he would show up—couldn't believe it until I saw his shape filling up my doorway, the shy grin that slowly grew on his face as he saw me, too.

It wasn't always easy to line up our schedules since, on top of working days that often went longer than ten hours, Roy worked a lot of weekends, too. I learned that not only did he work projects with the landscaping business he contracted with, but he also took on home contracting projects of his own, especially as the winter came on. But it helped immensely that his energy seemed inexhaustible. One night he came over for dinner after working—he later admitted—from 6 AM to past 6 PM that day, yet still he seemed as keen and restless as ever. It also helped that he had a car, which meant that unlike me, he didn't depend on bus schedules and the vagaries of accessible cabs.

Once or twice, I offered to go over to his place instead, but he reacted with a vague, uncomfortable demurral. I thought over his reaction several times, and couldn't help taking it to mean both that his apartment wasn't accessible, and that he was embarrassed that that was the case. But really it could have been a lot of things: was he a secret slob, for example? I had to catch myself before I tumbled too far down the dizzying path of "what would that mean if we lived together…"

On nights when we couldn't see each other, we quickly fell into a habit of—to my great surprise—phone calls. It didn't surprise me that Roy wasn't much into texting and used it for only the most perfunctory communication (emails likewise), but it did surprise me, all things considered, that he'd prefer calls over texts. Quietly I slotted it away with the assemblage of the other little preferences and quirks that continued to shape my impression of him as being strangely old-fashioned, courtly.

It didn't take long for me to realize that being on the phone actually made his speech more fluent, at least with me. I wondered if he found eye contact and all the other feedback of face-to-face speech overwhelming. Not that phone calls made him any more talkative, by any stretch of the imagination, and I wasn't comfortable just monologuing at him, as much as he seemed to enjoy it. So we often shared little more than a "hey," a quick exchange of impressions from our days—for him, often a bit of tricky engineering he was proud of having pulled off, or an amusing/exasperating client—and a closing "good night."

But it felt warmer and more genuine than texting, I found. I often felt afterwards as if I had been hugged, and went to bed smiling to myself. I savored the phrases he'd passed onto me, the comfortable rumble that his voice sank to when he wasn't bothering to project at all.

"You're looking peppy lately," my coworker Francis remarked to me, maybe a week and a half out from when I'd met Roy. A burly guy about my age, with a shaved head and a beard magnificent both in its density and redness, he sat across from me in our shared working space. "Lotsa smilin', good viiiibe..." Francis wasn't actually from California, but had gone to a UC for undergrad, and had never lost the attitude.

I was speechless with embarrassment at first. I leaned forward and rubbed my hand through my hair, partially shielding my face from him.

Francis raised his eyebrows—also impossibly red. "Got something really good going, huh? Exotic juice diet? Sick workout regime?"

I laughed and rolled my eyes. "You know me and the workouts. No, I..." I paused. "I'm seeing someone and it's going well, actually." Normally at work I was reserved about my private life, but I didn't feel like I could come up with a convincing lie at the time; nor did I want to. It wasn't hard for me to admit to myself that really, I wanted to tell *everyone* about Roy. Knowing that Francis was a talker, but not a gossip, helped.

Francis inclined his head, made a "respect, brother" kind of facial expression. "Congrats, dude. Glad to hear it. Keep killin' it." He didn't ask for further detail; I bobbed my head and said thanks; he returned his attention to his work.

Given that our department was on the younger side, a lot of people tripped over themselves to be progressive, and I'd certainly dropped strategic hints about my sexual orientation on occasion. But I didn't feel secure enough in either my level of out-ness or the duration of my relationship with Roy to start going into detail just then. Even though I trusted Francis, unlike a decent number of others at the company I knew, to be above immediately instigating long sessions of speculation about how exactly a dude with one working limb could do it with another dude. God! The thought made me nauseous.

***

That weekend, Amy and I had lunch together, at her place. When I rang her doorbell, she was so eager to see me that even from outside I could hear her stomping across the kitchen floor. The door opened; Amy's face, haloed with her short, bouncy, coppery-bright curls, practically blazed with excitement; her pale blue-grey eyes looked electric. "Asher!" She leaned on one of her forearm crutches and let the other hang as she bent to give me a hug. "Hey, Gams," I said happily into her shoulder.

Amy and I had met at a summer camp for teens with CP and other muscle disorders, when I was just about to go into junior year of high school, and she had just finished hers. Her family had just moved to the area—a tough transition heading into the final year of high school—and had enrolled her in the camp to help her feel more at home. I'd been attending the camp since the beginning of high school, and had made a number of good friends there—several of whom I was still in touch with—but no one had clicked like Amy and I had. It was like fire meets fire, in a good way: we were both hyperanalytical chatterboxes, so we could bounce off of each other and make abstruse jokes for hours. We kept a spiral notebook we called "The Laboratory," detailing thought experiments we'd run together: convoluted sequel pitches for favorite movies, national economies based on monetization of low-probability weather events, that kind of thing. Even in retrospect it still made me laugh more out of genuine amusement than out of embarrassment at how clever we thought we were.

Like me, Amy had spastic CP, but only her legs were affected, and though her knees and feet, too, were contracted, she was quite mobile and could stomp around beautifully with braces and crutches—hence my nickname of "Gams" for her. I had briefly been "Wheels," not surprisingly, but it was too obvious to stick. And "Gams" suited Amy in more way than one—she was really quite gangly, would have been taller than me if I could stand up, which added to her general air of expansive, breathless, slightly madcap energy. Being around her made me feel as if I'd just had a shot of espresso.

"Asher," she said pleadingly as she led the way inside, pausing to use one crutch to knock a stray pair of boots out of the path, "I've been *so* good."

"You *have* been so good," I said, laughing. "I think you sent me only like fifty more question marks yesterday."

"I could have sent you fifty-one, or used up all of your data with videos of cats falling over or something. So, *am* I going to get to hear more about this guy today? What you've told me so far is like barely more than what Google told me, which is that... he has a 4.75-star rating on a home contracting site."

"You Googled him?!" I was mortified.

"Come on, that's just common sense nowadays—I'm serious," she said, turning to glare at me when I laughed awkwardly, "it's obviously what anyone should do."

"Okay, okay." I had Googled him myself, of course, but still felt chastened by the lengths to which Amy was going to look out for me.

Dinner was already on the table—Indian take-out, since Amy was far from domestic. We set to without any formality. "If you got out more, you'd be more savvy about this stuff," she said reprovingly, peeling open a tinfoil packet of naan. "It's even more embarrassing for you that you *have* a degree in comp sci."

"Yeah, well, this year was supposed to be my big coming-out, and we all know how that went." I had told her about squeamish James from Grindr, and she was well informed on all the dead ends that had preceded him. Collectively she deemed them ableist shitheels. I grimaced at her both illustratively, and because my legs were starting to spasm, pushing my feet against the footplates and my hips out of my chair, straining against my seatbelt. "But yes, anyway, I promised, so I *will* tell all tonight. Or at least most."

"No, all!" Her eyes glinted devilishly.

I turned my attention from my legs, operating as usual according to the laws of another dimension, in order to pick up my fork and point it at her, while delivering a quelling glare.

And then, over the course of dinner, I *did* tell her pretty much all—more than I'd told myself I would. I couldn't help it, I wanted to share with Amy, knew that she would help me puzzle it out, put things in a new light, resettle the pieces back into myself, with affection and enthusiasm.

The most glaring omission I made: I did not tell her about the men in the alleyway. Even though it was Amy, even though Roy had all but literally hand-held me through the crime report, I still felt as if I couldn't even talk to myself about what had happened. The thought of having to hold someone else's anger, horror, anything, was purely overwhelming. (Likewise —despite our weekly phone calls, I still hadn't been able to tell my parents, which filled me with shame.) So, Roy made a vaguer, less extravagantly dramatic, but still serendipitous entrance onto the scene as someone I "just met" on my way home after the disappointing James-date.

But I told her a lot about Roy. Not everything, not the details about him that felt so precious and intimate that I couldn't bear exposing them, as much as part of me wanted to shout them to the world, like how he looked when he was sleeping, or what it felt like to unexpectedly feel the weight of his hand on one of my shoulders. But I tried to share with her the outline, the silhouette of him I was slowly filling out in my mind: his intensity, his habitual solitude, his sometimes bewildering sweetness, his preference for physical expression.

On this last point, Amy was fascinated. "I admit," she said, leaning back in her chair—we had finished eating by that point —"I never imagined you with, like, He-Man."

"I know! Isn't it bizarre?"

"Not in a long-term way, at least," she continued. I restrained myself from asking her whether she thought we had long-term potential, because I didn't want to hear the answer. She was staring up at the ceiling with her hands behind her head, a slight frown crinkling her long, pale brows. I rubbed my right hand and wrist anxiously, pressed back slowly against the contracture, then slid my hand down to press against the tension in that elbow.

Amy sat up again and looked directly at me. "And you guys haven't done anything yet?"

I knew what she meant. "No. Is that weird, two weeks in?"

"It's not just 'two weeks in,' but you've been seeing each other a *lot* during those two weeks... Not even like, just a little bit of fooling around? I know you smooch and spoon a lot—" I grinned involuntarily, and she smiled, the distinctive lines around her eyes deepening, "—but nothing handsy?"

"No," I admitted. Roy had never gone further than the massage he'd given me on the first night he'd come over—but I dearly wished he would.

There had been times, many times, when I'd been tempted to start something, but in those moments I might as well have lost all remaining motor function; I shrank inside myself, nervous, overwhelmingly conscious of my inexperience, and of my imperfect, ungraceful body. Next to mine, Roy's body seemed to burn with potency.

I had woken up one morning to see him already awake and shirtless in the hallway, bouncing lightly from foot to foot, staring fixedly ahead at, I realized, his reflection in the bathroom mirror. His fists were raised. He darted back and forth, his bare feet weaving an intricate pattern on the floor, making soft scuffing noises; he ducked once, then threw a quick volley of punches at an invisible opponent. He was shadowboxing, I realized, a term that had never had physical meaning to me before.

He looked perfect, like a wild animal. Pure capability, pure motion. For some minutes I watched him in silence, until my arm started spasming, thudding my wrist against my chest, bringing me back to myself, and to a fuller realization of what I looked like, next to Roy.

"Okay..." Amy said, looking at me thoughtfully again. I pulled myself out of that memory, out of the self-pity. "There are a ton of things that neither you nor I know here, which makes it hard for me to say what might be weird or not. But here's my take. I *do* think it's unusual, given how you say he looks and acts, the physical energy, that he hasn't tried to move things forward with you. The fact that he *probably* hasn't been with a disabled guy before, I have to assume that's making him more cautious, it can't not.

"There's also the fact that you undoubtedly read to him as inexperienced. Sorry, babe, you know it's true."

"Guilty as charged." I raised my hand. "Or, you know, virginal."

"So, that's two big reasons not for him to go in, uh, guns blazing, as it were." She paused so we could both make retching faces, until she sobered up again. "And it *does* make me like him that, from what you've said, he's been bending over backwards to be respectful that way.

"But I think one thing you need to keep in mind is, he could be seeing other people. I'm not saying he is! But it could be the case." I'd known she was working her way up to a difficult point, but my stomach still sank at the suggestion, and my legs stirred again. The phrase "getting it elsewhere" flashed through my head, the phrase she'd be too diplomatic to ever use. She paused for a little while to let me work through my thoughts, before saying, "And, you know, it would be fine, right *now*, if he were seeing other people, because it's not like you guys have discussed anything about that yet. Right?" I shook my head in confirmation; I admitted to myself that the need hadn't even occurred to me. "But I just—I want you to be ready to protect yourself if you have to, Asher. You know, emotionally."

I thought for a while longer, trying to ignore my still-misbehaving legs, which were now "jogging" against my footplates. I tried to take the good Amy was offering—her brand of sensible, sardonic steeliness—and set aside the defensive hurt, the skittering anxieties. I looked up at her. "I'll try to keep my eyes open. Thanks, Amy. You're the best."

Finally she smiled again, and blew me a kiss from across the table. "Have fun. Play safe. And pleeease make sure I get to meet him if things roll along much further."

I hurried to agree, and after that she gently disengaged from the subject, moved toward lighter chat; I followed her gratefully, though part of me would have liked to pepper her with a dozen anxious questions.

After dinner, she walked me to the door without her crutches. "Hey," I said indignantly as I followed her, "you never even gave me time to ask about you and Vikram." Vikram was her boyfriend of over half a year; the last update I'd received had suggested they were getting quite serious, more serious than was habitual for Amy.

"Now you know it feels to want the juicy, juicy deets and not get, babe," she said over her shoulder as she lurched the last step to the door, catching herself with one hand before shuffling back slowly to pull the knob open. I wondered if things had gone awry, hoped they hadn't; her evasiveness could mean a lot of things, like she didn't want to talk about it *because* it was getting serious. As straight-shooting as she was, Amy could be remarkably enigmatic about her own business. She continued, one eyebrow raised, "Dinner, your place, next week?"

"It's a deal," I said as I rolled out. "Thanks again, Amy. Really."

"Make good decisions!" she yelled as I pulled out onto the sidewalk. It was pleasantly crisp outside, with a half-moon rising in a sky of a vibrantly deep blue. It was the first of November. I had a lot to think about.

8

Past is Present

That Sunday afternoon, Roy and I met up at the public library. I'd wanted to pick up a few new books I was excited about, and we'd agreed that a walk in neighboring Crown Hill Park sounded like a good idea afterward.

A curious thing happened on the way out. We were rolling out through the front lobby, Roy's footsteps and those of other patrons echoing off the polished stone around us, and before I could hit the handicapped button for the double set of glass doors out front, a man started holding the first set open for me.

He was striking: almost Roy's height, lean, swimmerish in build, with sandy hair, a wide mouth, and an eyebrow piercing. As I turned to say "thank you," I looked him over, as you do, but his pale, cattish eyes had already moved behind me and up to Roy. I saw his brows lift slightly in recognition. Then his eyes moved down to Roy's hand, which he had rested lightly on one of my shoulders, and the pierced eyebrow flicked up fractionally. "Hey," he said to Roy. The slight smile on his lips was hard to read.

Behind me, Roy said nothing. Belatedly, the man said "you're welcome" to me as we moved out through the first set of doors; Roy leaned around me to hit the button for the second set, still silent. I resisted the temptation to look behind me at the man.

We emerged into brilliant sunshine. The library's steep front steps led out onto a stone plaza still set up with café tables and chairs, and beyond that, the initially gentle, eventually precipitous slope of Crown Hill Park, threaded with winding, paved paths. The white belvedere that topped the hill, itself topped with a tiny American flag, looked absurdly picturesque in the bright sunshine, surrounded by half-bare oak trees and strolling parkgoers.

The view did a good job of distracting me from the man who'd held the door. I felt a freshness move through me. I looked up to my left, where Roy had stepped forward next to me: he seemed to feel similarly, rocking back on his heels with a slight smile lifting the corner of his mouth. Then he swept his gaze over the two flights of steps down, and the long, switch-backed wheelchair ramp to one side, deeply sunken within concrete walls. "Race you?" he said to me, his smile deepening.

I gave a snort of laughter. "Oh, come on, how is that even fair? I'm locked in to like four miles an hour here."

He looked at the steep stairs again. "I'll go backwards," he said decisively.

I opened my mouth to say something, stopped, raised my eyebrows, and said instead, "You're on. 'Three-two-one' and then on 'go'?"

Roy's face lit with a rare grin. My heart flipped in my chest.

I began the countdown. "All right—three, two, one, *go.*"

Roy burst into a sprint towards the steps, startling a middle-aged couple, each laden with an armful of books, who were about to enter the library. "Sorry!" he twisted around to exclaim at them as they recomposed themselves fussily, like small birds. Meanwhile, I had jammed my hand down on my joystick, but could hardly have claimed to have leapt into motion; when Roy was already a couple steps down, jogging backwards with one hand lightly on the railing, his eyes locked on me, I was just hitting the ramp's initial incline. By the time I was about to round the first switchback, I was close to doubled over in laughter at the sight of him bouncing backwards down the stairs, staring with wide-eyed intensity at me—the thing was, I genuinely couldn't tell if he was faking it—and oblivious to the variously amused and skeptical looks of the library patrons passing by in either direction.

I emerged from the final slope to find Roy jogging determinedly in place on the last step. He watched carefully to see when my wheels hit level, and only then did he deliberately step down onto the ground. He turned to me and thrust both arms up in the air to mime "winner!" on my behalf.

We kissed in full sight of a gaggle of passing teenage girls, who watched with wide eyes and immediately turned to whisper to one another. I closed my eyes.

"Temporary gravitational sinkhole got ahold of you?" I inquired as we broke.

"Must be," he said. "Damnedest thing. They should have that s-step looked at." We kissed again, and then moved off into the park.

***

It was much later in the afternoon before I dared to ask Roy, "So who was the guy in the library?" We were sitting side-by-side near the top of Crown Hill, Roy on a park bench, massive arms and legs sprawled out in the sun, me pulled up alongside the bench.

He picked his head up from the back of the bench and looked at me blankly. He looked slightly sun-dazed; it was remarkably warm for November.

I tried not to get distracted by his heavy-lidded gaze. "The guy who held the door for us," I said, succeeding, I thought, in keeping my tone light.

He looked blank for another moment, before a grim cast came over his face. He immediately sat up, put his legs together, and dropped his chin to his chest. I wondered for the tenth time whether he was aware of how legible his body language always was; I was only surprised that he hadn't crossed his arms.

"Someone I used to sss... ss... spend time with," he said finally.

I wasn't sure what to say. I was relieved of the choice between either a further diplomatic inquiry or a breezy, falsely unconcerned "oh" when he continued, "I shhhh... should w-warn you that I used to be..." his head dropped further towards his chest, both in thought and, I expected, with the effort of working around his stutter, "...pretty p-p-promiscuous for a www... while."

He was growing visibly frustrated, and hunched over for a silent quarter of a minute, his mouth working soundlessly, one hand tapping hard against his leg.

Finally he was able to continue: "Jjjjj... just for about a year, when I was m-much yyyy-yuh-younger. But... what happened at the library—th-that may not be the last t-time that hhhh... happens." He shook his head sharply once at the end, as if trying to exorcise himself. A college kid walking by with a dog looked at Roy curiously, then looked away quickly when he saw me noticing, only to look back again to give my wheelchair a once-over. That time, I pretended not to notice.

I let out a breath. "Thank you for telling me," I said to Roy, again succeeding, I thought, in maintaining an even tone. I felt slightly detached, out-of-frame with the sunny afternoon around us, the sounds of laughter and idle conversation, the occasional hum of weekend traffic. Roy had leaned forward onto his forearms and interlaced his fingers, holding them tightly and stiffly, and looked between them at the ground.

I had, I realized, been projecting the image of a certain kind of midcentury gay man onto him—secluded, furtive, his life ruled by an unspoken intensity and punctuated by sexual encounters that were as scarce as they were ferocious. I had, it had to be admitted, also gotten off several times imagining such desperate back-alley encounters, feat. Midcentury Roy.

It was true that Roy's conversation was noticeably absent of any mention of past relationships—none of the "this guy I used to date" that tended to come up easily in the conversation of twenty- and thirty-somethings. It confounded me now that I had been ready to imagine few, or even no, serious relationships and a little casual sex—but not a *lot* of casual sex. I felt almost sickened by my own naiveté.

Roy was looking at me now, searching my face anxiously for a reaction. "I'm not sure what to say," I said, finally. I liked to think of myself as an honest person, but it cost me, it pushed me whenever I had to admit that I was feeling anything less than one hundred percent positive about something. "I'm a little out of my depth with this. I think I've pretty much said this before, but in case it wasn't clear, I have never... been in any kind of relationship before, anything beyond a little flirting." Roy nodded. "So I apologize if I say anything that sounds... dumb, or judgmental—and you should tell me if I do. But I'd really like to ask you some more questions. Is that okay?" He nodded again, his brows furrowed.

I started rubbing the tops of my thighs with my gloved hand, partly because I was getting chilly as the sun descended, partly to burn off nervous energy. At least I hadn't started spasming.

"How do you feel about that time in your life?" I said after a pause.

He grimaced, then unlaced his hands and sat up to face me more fully. He gestured roughly towards his mouth: "Not guhhh... gonna be g-good," he warned me. I nodded. "B-but I'm nnn-not yyy-using it t-to... get out of talking to y-you."

I was aghast. "I would never think that."

He shrugged, and I had to wonder how many times he had been accused of that before.

We both sat back and looked further down the hill, where the college kid I'd noted before was now keeping his gleefully zig-zagging dog occupied with the help of a tennis ball and another guy. I briefly, wistfully, wondered if the two guys were dating.

"It w-wasn't a guhhh... g-good time," Roy said beside me. "Th-there were a ffff... f-few years when I was a-angry all—all the time. The sss-sex phase came ttt... tuh... toward the end of it. For a while I thought I was just h-having fun, that I was happier. I think ssss... s-sometimes I was. But mostly it was a way of—" he mimed angrily shoving something away from himself. I nodded, and reached out to take one of his hands without thinking about it. He looked at my hand with genuine surprise, as if it had come from somewhere else entirely, and then paused, giving me a grateful look. As usual, his hand was ungloved, chilled, and made mine feel absurdly small when he squeezed.

"I sss-ss–*stopped* after I had some... health scares." I flinched, and the pit of my stomach sank. "Not... the big one," he said, seeing my face. I relaxed, a little. "B-but I was stupid enough that it took more than one sss... s-scare for me to actually stop.

Th-the fact that I didn't stop af... afff... *after* one, when I cleared my head, th-that told me how b-bad it had rrrr-rr-really gotten.

"Around then—was also when I s-started boxing. That helped a lot to—get me out." He arced his free hand, mimed it rising over a barrier and landing in another space.

He stopped then, seemingly exhausted. I was genuinely getting cold now, I realized, and my legs, arm, and back were contracting in response, the familiar pain pulling through muscle and joints, setting me slightly askew in my chair. But I didn't want to interrupt the conversation.

On the hillside below us, the dog was lolling on its side in the grass, as the two guys rubbed its white belly from either side. Good living.

Roy took my hand in both of his and stroked it gently with his thumbs. He was staring off over his right shoulder; the sun was drawing close to setting behind the hill in that direction. Everything around us was tinted a heavy gold; his slightly grown-out stubble glinted.

After a time, I said, "Thank you for telling me. I really appreciate your honesty. This is... a lot for me to think about. But I'm sorry that you felt so much... so much pain and anger." Dimly, I was aware that I was already getting ready to shy away, to seal off the conversation with kindness and courtesy when I could have, and partly wanted to, push ahead, know more, ask more. But I felt unequal, I was flinching away, just as when I longed to touch him more, and didn't.

From the queasy swirl of anxiety, fearful curiosity, shame (whose shame?) inside myself, I fished up a distinct thought: *Coward. Ask him another question.*

I went for the most immediate: "Can I ask—was the man at the library anyone in particular?"

"His name is Cyrus," Roy said with surprising immediacy, and a strange emphasis, as if the name spoke for itself. I could look at his eyes because he wasn't looking at me; they were tense, slightly narrowed. If anything, he looked angry. "He was ppp... parrr... part of the bad sssside of things. I don't talk to him anymore," he said crisply, swinging his head around to look at me again.

I held myself against the impulse to flinch away from his gaze. "The bad side of things," I repeated, without really knowing what I was saying.

His eyes slid away to the side, and he made an ambiguous noise, a *hmmm* that could have been agreement, frustration, or a signal that more was to come. After a moment he returned his gaze to me and said, "I don't t-t-talk to anyone from that time anymore, don't ggg... go looking." There was no more anger in his face, just—I thought—a serious desire for me to believe him. And then he gave a hint of a smile and said, "I'm ggg... gg... *good* at not talking to pp-people." At the end he lifted his eyes to me in a way that implied *other than you.*

I smiled reluctantly, gently freed my hand from his to run it through my hair, and then pushed myself to the left to off-set the rightward skew of my back. I hated it when my back spasmed, even more than when my arm or legs did. It was the loss of control, on top of the pain; I felt as if I'd tip over if someone gave me a hard-enough push.

I kept my good hand on the opposite armrest so I could keep the sensation of bracing myself. All of the physical sensation, the involuntary jerks and slow contractions everywhere but my good arm, I used it now as a distraction to drown out the second-guessing and buzzing nervousness. I pushed myself to just talk through all of it.

"Roy, I want you to be happy. And I want to be part of that. It hurts me when I've seen things like this that seem to say... that say that you were hurting yourself. I'm scared trying to talk about this because I have no way of... knowing what any of that would be like, I don't have a way of seeing into that kind of... experience.

"I don't even know if you feel like you *need* me to be able to understand that about you. But I do want to."

I paused, looked to him for a response, still bracing myself against my right armrest.

He was hunched over his knees, twisting to look back at the sunset again, but nodding slowly at what I said. "What do you need from me?" he said finally, simply.

I felt a deep and immediate sense of gratitude, which was quickly stained with guilt. "I need to know that I can trust you," I admitted.

He nodded to himself again, and then looked back at me and nodded once more, more deeply this time. His lips were compressed.

I think we both felt that we had said everything we could say in that moment. Nothing felt closed; everything hung around us. It felt harder but also more truthful than if we had attempted to reach any kind of conclusion.

Finally, Roy reached out his hand for mine again. As quickly as I could, I pulled it off my armrest to extend it to him. (My back was maybe, maybe relaxing again.) Exhaling, he held onto my hand, hung his head.

I couldn't stand him looking so abject. I shook his hand until he looked up at me, and I gave him a smile. I glanced over his shoulder—"Propriety police incoming," I said. Approaching us there was a large family with a father whose gaze was pinned on us, face screwed into such a sour expression that he looked like the Judginess addition to the line-up of Greek Comedy and Tragedy masks.

Roy glanced back, turned to me with his eyebrows lifted and one corner of his mouth edging upward. On an unspoken cue, just as the family drew level with us, we leaned forward and kissed. From the disagreeable patriarch, there was an audible gasp.

I doubted either of us would normally have gone for exhibitionism for the sake of it, but the mood needed to break. As the family hurried by under the patriarch's wing, we shared a silent laugh. The air seemed to clear a bit, until I just felt sore and chilled, no longer anxious to the point of near-nausea.

I became aware that the sun had entirely disappeared below the crest of the hill. There were deep shadows around Roy's eyes, under his cheekbones.

"Roy?"

He looked at me curiously, without a trace of wariness. I felt a little surge of gratitude again. *I* can *trust you*, was my immediate thought, unfair or not, unwise or not.

"I was going to ask... can I go with you to your boxing gym? Sometime soon?"

He tipped his head back slightly, startled. It took a moment before he said, "Shh-sure. Th-that could be fun."

The way he said "fun," I hoped he wasn't overestimating either my willingness or ability to actually participate in... anything. "Just tell me before the next time you go, okay?" I said. I wondered what I was getting myself into, but I was desperately eager now to see into this part of his life.

He abruptly stood and held his hands out to me. The way he was looking at me, I think he would have picked me up by my hands and swung me, if he could have—if I could have. "Let's go," he said. "You're cold."

The way he was looking at me was intoxicating. I smiled gratefully at him and pushed down on my joystick. He fell into place alongside me, running his hand up my arm until it rested on my shoulder. Around us, blue shadows grew.

About halfway down the hill, Roy suddenly stepped back and dropped to his hands in the grass to one side. There he did about twenty push-ups in rapid succession. I watched, bewildered and fascinated by the display of what I guessed was some sort of high spirits. Roy bounced up to his feet again, breathing heavily and shaking grass off his hands. His eyes shone strangely in the twilight, and he was grinning a little.

"I could do that too if I wanted to; but I'm so above it," I said languidly, and propped my chin on my hand in a superior attitude. I only wished I could cross my legs for additional effect.

He gave a gust of laughter, bouncing slightly from foot to foot, a big man acting like a boy. He had so much *energy*.

Do you feel free now? I wanted to ask him, but didn't. I couldn't help feeling that a burden had been passed on to me.

Still, I looked at him in the twilight, and knew that I loved him.

9

And the Night Came On

Shortly after the day at the park, when I had started to tell Asher about the worst of my past, we were sitting on his couch together, doing not much. I had been asking him about the book he was reading, one of the ones we'd picked up together from the library, when his phone rang.

He picked up, frowning slightly when he saw the number. "Hello?"

I could hear a woman's voice on the other end.

"Yes, this is Asher Klein," he confirmed, a little warily.

I watched as he listened for a little less than a minute. I couldn't make out more than the occasional word. Asher's face got tenser; I could see that he was steeling himself. "Yes. Okay. Okay, I see. No—okay, yes, I think I understand. Great. Yes, thank you. Have a good morning."

He exhaled hard when he hung up, and paused for a moment before turning to me, tilting his head back a little to look up at me—even sitting, the difference in our heights was significant. Asher had mentioned once that his doctors were sure he'd have been small even if he hadn't had CP. "They've arrested all three of the men from the alleyway," he said, his voice carefully even.

I felt a hot, vindictive flare of triumph. "That's amazing," I said. I reached out to hug him, but his slight frame felt resistant in my arms, stiff.

"Apparently Mr. William Riley was easy, thanks to your quick thinking with the wallet," he said, muffled, from inside my embrace, as if I hadn't done anything. "And one of the other guys was easy. But it took them a while to scrape up the last one." I withdrew my arms from him, and he looked up at me again. "Apparently they have another 'associate' who has a really similar name and appearance, which confused things. Who knew there were even more of the bastards?" He said it without smiling.

I put my hand on his upper arm. "How are you feeling?" I would have liked to jump up and punch the air in celebration, but it was clear that he was struggling. I reined myself in.

"I'm not sure," he admitted. "I guess I should feel relieved, but I just feel... blank. Weird."

"Y-you wish it all hadn't happened," I offered; he had more or less said as much, during a conversation we'd had when I'd had to wake him up from a nightmare some time ago.

"Yes," he said, still flatly. But he leaned into me, now, pressing his weight against my side. Again I put my arms around him, ran a hand up and down the thin, taut length of his right upper arm, the bent one. This was why I loved it when he decided to take the effort to transfer to his couch, we could just *be* next to each other. Although seeing him sitting without his wheelchair had been weirdly disorienting for me at first, the way it made him look exposed. On a basic level, I had the sense that if he wanted to go somewhere, he should be able to do that, and not being in his wheelchair was the opposite of that. I had to remind myself that it really didn't take him that long for him to transfer. And, I had learned, it was important for him not to be in his wheelchair for too long, to keep changing up how his weight was distributed.

I rested my chin on the top of his head now. "So what happens next?" I said gently.

He took a breath. "They'll be arraigned in about two weeks, on charges of attempted theft, and assault." He stumbled over it a little bit, when he tried to say "assault." "We may be called in before then to provide additional evidence, again."

We had already gone to the police station once together to provide additional statements in support of the written crime report. (And to drop off the wallet.) Asher had been miserable the whole time, pale, spasming almost continuously, which had been wrenching for me to see—and I had had to hold myself back from comforting him the way I longed to.

Afterward, it had taken him hours to calm down again. That night had been the one when I'd had to wake him up after he started whimpering and struggling in his sleep. (My heart clenched again, thinking about the sounds he'd made, how long it had taken him to recognize me after I'd been able to wake him.)

But I had believed so much in the *rightness* of what we were doing at the police station, what we were trying to have done, that I had been able to make it through with barely any stuttering, carried through by a furious momentum, the same that I felt now.

Again, I reminded myself to be still, gentle, to listen and watch carefully.

"After the arraignment, we'll hear back about how they decided to plead, all three of them," Asher concluded.

"So it could all be over in t-two weeks," I said encouragingly. Reluctantly, he nodded against my shoulder, his curls rustling.

He pushed himself back slightly then. "Wanna hear something funny?" he asked. It was clear he was making an effort to make his tone lighter. An idea that had been forming in my head over the past few weeks was that one reason that we got along was because we'd both had to develop a strong sense of something like contempt for self-pity. Another idea that followed was that in this case, that same sense of contempt was making it harder for Asher to actually deal with his reaction to everything that had happened in the alleyway. But that idea was too cloudy still for me to feel comfortable saying anything about it.

I brought my attention back to his half-smiling face. "Hm?"

"The officer who called? It wasn't someone we saw at the station. She said her name was Officer Ruby. Isn't it funny that she would call herself "Officer" plus her first name? It just sounds like a character in a kid's cartoon show. Like, she would definitely have bright red hair, in a ponytail."

I paused. "Isn't it much more l-l-likely that her *last* name was Ruby?"

His mouth opened slightly. "Well, shit."

Finally, he relaxed, releasing a torrent of incredulous laughter; it sounded only slightly hysterical. I held him tighter, smiling into his hair.

When his laughter had run its course, he mumbled into my arm, "That was such a stupid mistake." Under my hand, his right shoulder jerked slightly.

I rubbed it. "It's okay. I'm sure she really did have r-red hair."

***

The night after Officer Ruby called, I awoke suddenly, which usually meant that I was going into spasm. My eyes flicked back and forth as I became slowly aware of several things, in succession.

First, I was *not* going into spasm.

Second, even through the blinds, the room was saturated with the blue glow of moonlight.

Third, I knew Roy was awake, too.

And he was very erect, and his erection was pressing hard against my hip.

I could tell he was awake from the extreme carefulness with which he was holding me. His tension was palpable; normally he surrendered his weight entirely as soon as he was alongside me. And his breath was irregular, as if he kept thinking about doing something and then interrupting himself.

I turned my head to face him. "Hey," I said softly. His head immediately jerked back, and he began the motion that he must have been poised to do, which was to roll away from me. He didn't do it fast enough for me not to see how guilty his face looked.

"Hey, wait," I said. My heart pounded, but I was proud that I was able to speak without my voice trembling. Slowly, he rolled back. "Do—do you want to?" He looked at me for a long moment. The moonlight made his eyes look unnaturally large, dark. Finally he said, his voice vibrating through the bed under me, "Well, do *you* want to?"

"Yes," I said, "of course." I had started getting hard as soon as I had woken up, maybe even before.

And I willed myself to move my hand to him. He gasped as I ran my hand lightly over his cock through his boxers—it was sized in accordance with the rest of him—and for an instant his eyes fluttered shut. I craned to kiss him—I couldn't push myself up, with my arm otherwise occupied—and he surged to meet me. He kissed me deeply, flicking out his tongue, and then suddenly he rolled and was above me, straddling me on all fours, his massive shoulders and arms forming a frame above me, black against the blue-lit room. He was still wearing his boxers, and I tugged at the waistband impatiently with my hand. I wanted to see him, feel him. He shifted to one side again to strip off swiftly—his cock sprang free, pointing toward me, thick, commanding—then returned to kiss me again, slid one hand down my belly and beneath the waistband of my own boxers.

At first he slid only his work-roughened fingertips there, lingered with torturous delicacy on the skin just above my groin, below my hipbones. I gasped, and he chuckled appreciatively against my lips. At the sound, the sensation, I grew even harder, my blood surging. His fingers teased the edges of my pubic hair.

I felt as if I were going out of my mind. Everything was pushed out of me but the hot pulse of desire.

His fingers slid far enough to feel the scars from when I'd had hip surgery; I knew he could feel them from the way that he paused over them.

Before I could feel self-conscious, he shifted his hand and slowly, slowly palmed my hard cock. I could feel a shudder run through him the first instant that he touched it. On it he rocked the length of his enormous hand from side to side, before sliding down further to stroke my balls.

The sensation was engulfing. I was starting to lose control of my arm and legs. My breath was ragged, desperate, I stroked and gripped his back and side and shoulders frantically with my good hand, as my contracted limbs began to twitch and struggle. I felt as if I had been disassembled; I couldn't string together a coherent thought, a coherent motion. Roy was now kneeling back, using both of his hands to stroke me, two fingers stroking under my balls, the other hand lightly running up and down my shaft. I couldn't see his face, or I couldn't focus to see it. His breath, too, was eager, panting.

My good arm fell back; for a moment all I could do was use it to grip the bedsheets, as if trying to hold something together. For an instant I saw myself as if from above, my contracted arm and hand beating meaninglessly across my chest, my legs kicking and jerking arrhythmically; I felt a distinct, piercing sensation of shame.

And then Roy's hands were around my face, warming, steadying. "Are y-you okay? Am I hurting you?"

I gasped again, this time at the loss of sensation, contact, from my cock. "No, no, *I need you*," I whispered. I was shaking.

A low sound rumbled through Roy's chest; he slid one of his hands aside from my face and pressed his lips to my jaw. "I love your body," he said, his voice thrumming through my jaw, my throat. And swiftly he kissed my shoulders, my hands, my chest, again and again. "It's so honest. It drives me crazy."

I couldn't do anything but struggle upwards to meet his lips; we kissed interminably. His hands moved again to my cock, and gratefully I felt their heat throbbing into me.

Then he broke the kiss, and I arched weakly and gasped as I suddenly felt his mouth on my cock, impossibly warm, wet. My legs kicked against his shoulders, massive, impervious, and I cried out as he began moving on me, my understanding of what was happening further splintering—the heat, the intensity of the pleasure, the impossible sweetness of it, his hand cupping my balls and stroking, the meaningless pain as my limbs struggled against themselves, the pain a hot wire running through everything else.

When I came in his mouth, I barely understood what was happening; my vision burst white, and my hips and abdomen convulsed. I cried out again.

As my vision cleared, I became dimly aware that Roy's mouth was still on me, that he was still gently, slowly moving his tongue against me. I thought I would die from the sweetness of it.

Slowly he released me, leaned forward to cup my face with one hand, that familiar gesture. I couldn't talk, but he looked deeply into my eyes, kissed my lips, leaving a trace of moisture. He sat back on his heels, tilting his face to the ceiling before closing his eyes and palming himself.

With drugged slowness, I moved my hand to meet his. His eyes flickered open again. He looked at me for confirmation; I managed a nod. He put his head to one side and smiled, gently placed my hand around his cock, and closed his over it. With our joint hands, he began stroking himself, swiftly; dimly I marveled at the sensation of my hand on him, the firmness, the velvety skin, the heavy shell of his hand around mine.

Half a minute or half an hour later, I couldn't have said, he came, shuddering and moaning. My eyes were closed then, but I felt a few warm drops drip down my fingers, fall from him to my abdomen. I could feel the bed shift as he fell forward heavily, twisting to curl up at my side.

My arm and legs had slowed, calmed, seemingly obeying an additional gravity. I had regained enough presence of mind that I could fight to slow my breathing, but I still felt as if I would never be able to move any part of my body voluntarily again. Slow heat pulsed through my core.

Roy moaned again, into my ear this time, softly. His hands moved across my chest until they had each found one of mine, took them, the crippled and the whole.

The last things I remembered before we fell asleep, both of us, were the sound of our breathing, and the feeling of his lips pressed against my neck.

10

Aftershocks

That morning, I woke up twice, the first time just around dawn. I lifted my head, looked around a bit. The outlines of Asher's room, the furniture, looked a bit ghostly, flat, in the greyish light. It must have been overcast outside. I felt blank, fuzzed out, myself. *What did I do?* said a blank, confused voice in my head; it sounded young. I ran a hand over my torso under the covers, found it tacky.

You had sex, said another voice: flat, accusatory.

I felt an automatic surge of sick heat in my gut. *Oh.*

Nausea, fear. Anger. I'd let someone down: myself.

I exhaled and pulled my hands out from under the covers, pressed the heels of my palms to my eyes.

Next to me, Asher stirred slightly as the draft slipped under the covers.

I was actually startled to be reminded of him. I snapped my head to the side, lowering my hands, to look at him. He was still deeply asleep. His head was tilted to one side on the pillow, his curls tossed back, his pale lips parted. The skin of his eyelids was so fine that I could see his veins through it, and a slight tremble of motion as his eyes moved in his sleep. I could see the top of his small hand, the bent wrist, just at the edge of the comforter, and without thinking about it, I moved one hand to cover it, feeling his warmth, his fine bones.

I relaxed. Carefully, I pushed anything resembling a thought out of my head. With nothing to feed it, the heat in my gut dwindled. I looked at Asher and held his hand until I fell asleep again, sliding down gradually as if beneath grey water.

When I woke up the second time, the light was brighter, but still grey. I guessed I'd fallen asleep for about an hour. This time I could tell that Asher was about to wake up because he was stirring slowly under the covers.

There was something I wasn't supposed to be thinking about. It seemed perfectly reasonable to let things keep running that way, so I didn't think. I just watched Asher until he woke up. It was as good as waiting for a sunrise.

Finally his eyes opened, and scanned the room gradually. Very, very slowly, he turned his head to look at me. "Hey," he said, and smiled. Warmth bloomed in my chest.

"Hey," I said, smiling back.

Asher started to pull his arm out from under the covers, but halfway through gave up and let it drop back heavily down between us. "I feel like a sack of potatoes," he said.

I snorted. "Cutest ss-sack of potatoes I've ever seen."

"Mm." He succeeded in pulling himself towards me a bit with his arm. "Hey," he said again.

I smiled even more, and gave him a kiss.

As I pulled back, he said, "Did you have a good time last night?"

I paused; I remembered what it was I wasn't supposed to be thinking about. I couldn't stop myself from recoiling slightly.

The look on his face was devastating. I felt as if there were tar in my belly, black, clinging, sour.

"Ssss... ss-sorry," I said, as soon as I could manage it. "I'm rr-really s-sorry. That wasn't about you. I puhhh... p-p... I promise." Fucking stutter.

Asher was clearly working to compose himself, his mouth open, his eyes flicking around, his bent right arm stirring against his chest. I reached out, took his left hand with both of mine. I coached myself: *Relax your mouth. Relax your jaw. Know that the stutter's there, but you can lean into it, slow it down, if you let yourself.* And I *moved* my mind back to everything I had felt, everything I had seen, last night: Asher's ecstatic smile as his head fell back against the pillow, the warmth of his body, his skin on mine, the rawness of his voice when he cried out. The frantic motions of his body, bewildering—when he'd first started shaking, I'd felt a deep stab of fear—yet deeply stirring. The nakedness of it. In one moment, it had struck me, it went through me with a shiver, that I was getting to see something, be part of something, about Asher that no one had ever seen before. I was getting to give him something new. I had felt flushed, rich with that knowledge.

I threaded words together in my head, over and over, until eventually I could say, carefully, "Asher, llll... last night was bb-better, even more m-meaningful than I could have imagined it bbb-being. Yyy-yuh-you mean so much to me. But... ss-sex comes www..." I had to pause again, breathing out with frustration. The words were there, piling up at the threshold of my mind, but it was as if I didn't know how to make them cross over into speech.

Finally I went on: "It's not s-s-straightforward for m-me anymore. I wish it w-wasn't like that. I hate myself rrrr... rr... right now for s-screwing up your morning. B-but please know —everything about last night w-was..." I searched for the right word. "It was precious to me. A-and if you ssss-s-see anything negative in me now... it's b-because of my own m-mistakes."

His eyes had moved back to mine after I'd said his name, and stayed there, as I struggled through what I had to say. At the end, he nodded, seriously. I could tell he had struggled to push down his reflexive hurt—but he had heard everything I had meant to say.

Slowly he said, "Is that why you waited?"

I had to think for a while, gently rubbing his hand between mine. I was grateful he hadn't withdrawn it; I wouldn't have blamed him if he had wanted to. "Mmm... mostly," I said. "I f-felt like... anything I wanted to do might hhhh... hurt you."

"You don't mean just physically."

I nodded, inexpressibly grateful that he understood. I mimed something smearing off of myself, squirming across to smear across him, too. He nodded in return, his eyebrows furrowed with concern.

His look renewed my sense of guilt; I almost wanted to turn away from the sincerity of his concern. "I'm s-sorry," I said again. "I really wanted this mm... morning to be for you."

His face softened, and despite everything, I felt a glow of pleasure, contentment, instantly rekindle inside me. "I love you," I said, before I knew what I was doing.

A hush seemed to come over the room. "I love you," he said.

We pressed our foreheads together. I felt his warm breath move out across my own lips as he exhaled.

We moved apart again. I ran a knuckle across his collarbone. "Do you sss... s-still feel like a s-sack of potatoes?"

He gave a startled laugh. "Yes, actually. Just so heavy, and warm."

"I've never seen your buhhh... body as... *soft* as you looked after you... f-finished," I admitted.

"Love is the best muscle relaxant," he offered.

I made a "can't tell whether I should actually laugh" face, and he laughed. "Then w-we should get you on a rr-regular prescription," I said after.

His smile faded slightly, the uncertain look returning. "But what about you?" he said.

"That'll take sss... some figuring out," I admitted. He gave me a prompting look, and I turned my head away on the pillow to think for a bit, during which he rubbed my jaw with his hand. It felt so good that I closed my eyes.

Mentally, I probed around carefully, testing which territories felt bad, which not-so-bad. I could see the beginnings of a conclusion.

Eventually I opened my eyes again. His hand on my face slowed, and he looked at me intently. "I think," I said carefully, "it mm... m-might help if I focus on y-you instead of me." He looked embarrassed, so I smiled with one side of my mouth, and then continued, "If I think about taking care of y-you, making things feel good for you. Sss—so it's—" I made a gesture as if I were cradling something.

"Hmm," he said. "So it's like... making a different kind of space?" I nodded eagerly. "One that doesn't have the same kind of associations, the bad ones?" Again, I nodded, and then dove to bury my face against his neck. "Hey!" he said, surprised, but clearly pleased.

"I'm just so hhh... happy," I said against his neck.

Asher laughed softly. "Let's keep it that way, okay? I don't want it to be like... everything is The Asher Show, 24-7."

"But taking care of you is more fun," I mumbled.

"You're such a *dude*," he said, laughing, reaching up to deliver a joking slap, really a tap, to the side of my face.

I gave an appropriate wince, and said complainingly, "I l-liked it buhh... *better* when you were a bag of potatoes."

This time he moved his arm into a chokehold around my neck, and squeezed gently until I poked my tongue out in submission. "Gotcha, you pig," he said. "Potatoes strike back."

The expected round of kisses and gentle tussling followed. I loved being able to run my hands all over his bare skin, toss him around in bed a bit, and he seemed to enjoy it just as much, laughing breathlessly when I lofted him into the air, launching him towards the foot of the bed. He bounced on the comforter as he landed, still laughing helplessly, his eyes closed. His bent legs kicked out repeatedly, and his right arm moved in short jerks. I had to savor the fact that it was still one of very few times that I'd seen that happen out of excitement, rather than stress. I followed him in a pounce, planting my hands on either side of his face and bending to bite one of his ears.

I was getting excited again. When Asher recovered from his laughing fit and looked up—and down—at me, he actually bit his lip. I almost jerked from the bolt of desire that ran through me. He moved his hand to my thigh, gave me a questioning look.

I had to pull back and think about it for a moment, blowing air out through pursed lips.

"I think," I said regretfully, "it would be bb... better to wait a bit more." I could still feel, in the pit of my stomach, that sticky uneasiness, the sense that I was waiting for something to reach up and grab me again, a familiar darkness that I was eager not to look into.

"Yeah," was all Asher said. I could see the regret in his eyes, the hunger, but also a kind of simple patience.

We shared a smile. And then I backed away from him— but was unable to stop myself from planting my hands on his thighs, still restlessly moving, and bending from there to press a kiss on the rosy-brown head of his cock. He moaned deep in his throat, and I could feel him twitch against my lips. I grinned as I pulled back and climbed off the bed. "Ss-soon," I promised.

"Better be," he said throatily.

"I'm guhh... going to go shower," I said deliberately.

He gave me a look, one that said, *Yeah, because you're so dirty*. I threw up my hands and strode away as he laughed on the bed behind me.

11

Bobbing and Weaving

There were steps into Roy's boxing gym. Just a short flight, three flights of pitted concrete before the dented metal door into the gym (which was clearly a repurposed industrial building, maybe a small warehouse)—but still, they were steps.

"I hope this isn't symbolic," I said, looking up at Roy.

He was sucking in his lower lip, thinking. His hand rested heavily on my shoulder. "I c-c-could probably lift you," he said, "but I think there's also a r-ramp in back, for equipment and stuff."

"Uhh... let's try that, please." I trusted Roy, but I was also already more nervous than I would have liked to admit, and not in the mood to try something even slightly questionable.

"I'm ss-sorry," he said, sounding suddenly miserable. "I thought I had thought this through, but obviously I didn't. I just... I got ttt... too excited just thinking about you vvv... visiting."

I couldn't help smiling, even though my heart was fluttering with anxiety. "We'll figure it out."

He led me down a narrow sidewalk to the left of the building—it was cracked and upheaved enough to jostle my chair and me. I winced when my chair lurched over a particularly bad crack, sending a painful jolt through my spine. Ahead of me, Roy walked fast, clearly a bit worked up, pushing aside encroaching branches of the dark, overgrown shrubs that lined the outer perimeter wall. I smiled again when he paused and stepped back to hold up a branch that would have been squarely at face level on me. "Thanks." He gave me back an uncertain smile.

I know we were both relieved when we made it past the gauntlet of shrubbery and into what turned out to be a small parking lot behind the building, and saw the long ramp leading up to the back entrance. Roy advanced, tested the door. "'S open," he said with relief.

"Great, great—"

The ramp led into a storage room, thankfully not too cluttered, and from there into the main gym. Thankfully again, nobody noticed when we came in, which gave me a minute to get my bearings, and steel myself.

This was, I had realized in the days leading up to my planned visit, the first time we would go anywhere together that would entail one of us meeting the other person's friends, and consequently the first time we might have to introduce ourselves as a couple. And we hadn't talked about how we wanted to handle it. Roy was so endearingly, childishly excited that I was coming to check things out that I honestly couldn't tell if he had thought that part through, either. The impression that I got, in this and other arenas, was that he was so used to operating solo, *and* mostly silently, that it was going to take him a while to update his sense of... not needing to explain anything to anyone. And for my part, I'd been too sheepish to bring it up.

Compounding all of this was the fact that I regarded anything resembling a jock—with the obvious and still baffling exception of Roy—with something close to terror. Along every single axis, they might as well have existed in a separate reality from me: nerd, Jewish, gay, disabled. The singular sports event I'd attended in my life—a college football game—my friends and I had talked through almost continuously, only making a token attempt to focus on the field when the rest of the crowd got excited about something, at which point we'd wave and cheer and laugh at our largely unsullied ignorance of anything going on.

All told, I had done my best to coax myself into a kind of breathless open-mindedness about how this visit would go. In practice, this meant that as Roy held the storage room's door open for me to roll into the main gym, I was about one-third terrified, one-third ready to be ironic and defensive, and one-third ready to be artificially friendly.

Roy was resting his hand on my shoulder again as we advanced, and I tried to draw strength from the warmth of the now-familiar gesture as I gazed around the gym. While I thought I could still get away with it, I briefly leaned my cheek to press against his hand, and he moved his thumb up to stroke gently.

The whole space had a distinctly dank, chilly smell, though caged metal fans overhead kept the air moving. I didn't think I'd be taking my coat off. The floors were concrete, with wide stretches of black rubber matting. The walls were painted white, peeling in spots. Overhead hung long strips of fluorescent lighting, casting an even but harsh light on the two rows of punching bags that hung from chains a few feet away from us, like oversized fruit—some the long heavy kind, black and impossibly dense-looking, others the plump little colorful ones. A compact man with his back turned to us was working out with one of the little ones, creating a constant, light, drumming rhythm as he struck it again and again in rapid succession, occasionally punctuated by a squeak from the chain.

Beyond the punching bags, there was an open matted space, and then a roped-off square platform around which maybe eight men in loose shorts and t-shirts were chatting, stretching, jogging in place. A few looked like college kids; the rest I guessed were over 30. In the way they were moving, in the way they were talking to each other, there was a general sense of easy camaraderie, but also a kind of teasing watchfulness or wariness, a playfully competitive edge.

Despite my rapid heartbeat, I found myself smiling.

Roy was looking down at me, his own smile growing in eagerness, his eyebrows lifted. He'd never been this excited to show me something before. "What do you think?"

"It's just like in movies. All-American."

He laughed in an embarrassed way.

In front of us, the man punching the little bag slowed, delivered one last blow with a theatrical wind-up, then turned to face us. I guessed he'd heard Roy's laugh. "There you are," he said.

I immediately liked him. He looked somewhere between 50 and 60, with a weathered, narrow face accentuated by a hawkish nose and grey beard with a few black streaks in it. A short-brimmed black cap was pulled low over his dark eyes. He stood with a wide-legged stance, shifting from foot to foot with the same kind of restlessness that I'd grown accustomed to in Roy, though he had a black elastic brace on one knee, and seemed to be favoring it slightly. All things considered, he looked like the kind of guy who'd play guitar in bars on the weekend, when he wasn't camping.

"Allan," Roy said with obvious warmth as the man headed down the aisle between the punching bags toward us. He exchanged a handshake/clap-on-the-shoulder combo with Roy, smiling slightly, then switched hands without hesitation to shake with me. It only cemented how much I already liked him: it took a lot of people a weirdly long amount of time to realize that I could only shake with my left hand.

"And your friend made it, too." His handshake was warm and impressively strong, his fingers large and knuckly, even though he wasn't all that much bigger than me.

I resisted the impulse to look up at Roy when Allan said "friend." What kind of "friend" had I been described as?

"Hi," I said automatically, "Asher."

"Asher," he repeated, with a slightly mysterious smile. *What did it meeeeeeeean...* Roy and I were going to have a talk after this, for my sanity's sake.

I maintained the smile on my face, hoping I wasn't as wide-eyed as I felt.

"Uh," Roy said, "if you dd-don't mind, Asher, I'm g-gonna go get started." He nodded his head in the direction of the men congregated around the boxing ring.

"Oh, of course," I said. "I'll just..."

"Allan was great and ppp... p-promised me he'd hang with you. He's really good at explaining stuff," Roy said eagerly.

"Getting over an injury," Allan added in an explanatory tone, when I looked back to him. "Not allowed to do much for the next month, so I'm mostly here to get out of the house and give guys like Roy—" he reached up to slap Roy's shoulder "—a hard time from the sidelines."

Roy ducked his head and grinned, then turned to lead the way towards the other end of the gym.

When the gazes of most of the other guys came to bear on us, I had to work to keep my face still. There was the usual assortment of raised eyebrows and ill-concealed double-takes when they saw me in my chair; I became aware that my heartbeat was pounding in my ears again. Of course, to complete the picture, my right leg started kicking repeatedly, and my arm contracted more tightly against my chest. Despite the chill, I was ready to break into a sweat as I rolled up toward that gathering of poised, athletic men. It didn't help my nerves that I could feel that Roy's attention wasn't really on me. I would have been mortified to have him worrying about me the whole time, but I could also, pathetically, have really used a hug then.

I took a deep breath.

With Allan at my side, I worked my way through a series of thankfully laconic introductions. I tried to feel reassured by the mixture of low-key friendliness and a general lack of overinquisitiveness. The question I'd been afraid of—some variation on "Why are you even here?"—didn't make an appearance, even in subtext; people seemed genuinely happy, or at least satisfied, that I was just there to check out what "my friend" Roy got up to in so much of his time off. There were even a couple of not-that-awkward offers of help if I "wanted to try anything out...", which I declined with an "oh, maybe next time" that I hoped sounded genuine, but not *too* genuine.

Only one of the guys made zero effort not to stare at my body, especially, I thought, my arm, which was still clenched against my chest. The rest, I decided I was ready to try to like.

The men were dispersing now into smaller groups, some heading for the bags, others for the open matted area, listening to a short, intimidatingly muscular man with thinning sandy hair who seemed generally In Charge. We hadn't been introduced, but I knew from previous conversation with Roy that that had to be Kemp, the gym's owner. In the open area, some of the guys grabbed jump-ropes, others were pulling on small padded fingerless gloves, nothing like the bulbous red gloves I was used to seeing in, say, photos of Muhammad Ali.

I settled back in my chair to watch as they began drills or exercises, and allowed myself to entertain a slim sense of having survived the worst. (And my leg spasms, at least, were subsiding, although my right leg was still winched a good way out of the seat, tilting me in the opposite direction.) I let out a breath with a puff that I realized a moment later would have been pretty audible. Allan caught my eye, raised an eyebrow inquiringly. I looked away, embarrassed that my nervousness must have been so obvious to him, then looked back and said a quick "Sorry."

"Hey, come on," he said. The easy humor—and the surprisingly, openly fond smile—with which he said it suggested that I was being too hard on myself.

I smiled back, broadly this time. "I'm surprised Roy hasn't talked about you more to me," I said. I liked him that much.

He let out a laugh and crossed his arms as he stood next to me, looking out over the practice floor. "Roy? Talking?" Then he made a *pfffff* sound.

"Glad it's not just me," I said, giving him a knowing smile.

He rocked his head from side to side. Then he said, "No, we do get along, Roy and me. I've managed to get him to tell me a fair bit about himself, over the years." My ears just about perked up. "I've been here *forever*, even before Kemp owned this place, was certainly here when Roy first joined. Heard a lot since then. Still a surprise when I heard he managed to find you."

"Um..." My face was hot. I lifted my hand from my joystick to press it against my mouth, and pretended to be intent on an older black man who was jump-roping ferociously, sweat beginning to glisten on his dark brown skin, whipping the cord with at least twice the speed as the college kid next to him. Up in the ring, two men in padded helmets had squared off to spar under the watchful gaze of Kemp; appreciative shouts were coming up from the men watching them. Meanwhile, Roy was warming up with one of the long punching bags. He was, I realized now, almost a head taller than almost every other man here. I watched him with a kind of distracted appreciation. Seeing him in a new context gave me another opportunity to recognize how handsome he was.

Allan wasn't going to let me go, though. He looked down at me until he forced me to catch his eye again. "Well, you know. He's put himself through some rough shit. I'd been waiting for him to find someone nice for a while."

I looked up at him and was too nervous to even force a smile; my bad hand was pressing hard against my chest, the fingers twitching in and out convulsively. Allan continued, unperturbed: "And I do mean it when I say 'put himself through.' Roy is a good guy, but he overdoes shit."

At that, I had to laugh. "I think," I said, "I'd been trying to admit that to myself for a while. It feels good to hear someone else say it. It's... it's hard not to see him as, like, this incredibly noble person. And he *has* been through rough stuff. But..." I wasn't sure what I wanted to say.

"You guys are both young," he said, without condescension. "And Roy *is* noble. It's a rare quality. So I feel confident calling it when I see it. But sometimes—he goes out of his way to make things hard for himself. I think he has a Puritanical streak. Mortification of the flesh, is it? Or is that Catholic? Whatever."

I was nodding, slowly. The sparring match had ended in some kind of embarrassing upset: one of the guys was bent over with his hands on his knees, shaking his head, while Kemp shook his shoulder in chastisement. Roy had joined the circle of onlookers now, though he stood slightly to one side, occasionally turning away to shift into an active stance and practice a series of punches.

"Can I tell you something else?" I asked Allan. I was conscious of the weirdly immediate intimacy of our conversation, the fact that I didn't even know anything, really, about Allan. I would have felt bad if I didn't get the sense that Allan, himself, was enjoying getting to discuss Roy. He was holding forth, a bit. The way he savored some of his phrases as he said them suggested that he'd been formulating them for some time.

"Shoot," he said. He was drumming his fingers against his upper arms, looking amused.

"I'm just... I'm gonna be really straightforward, if you don't mind. I've never had someone to actually talk about Roy with, someone who actually knows him."

He gave an encouraging, almost impatient nod.

"I don't... Sometimes I feel confused by the fact that in most people's eyes, probably, I'm worse off—" I nodded my chin down at my body, my wheelchair "—but it feels like Roy actually has a lot more shit to work through. It's like my brain wants to reconcile those two pieces of information, and it can't. Is that stupid?"

I still wasn't quite sure I'd said what I was *really* chewing on, but that seemed to at least be in the neighborhood. I looked up, watched as Allan made a considering expression, pulling the corners of his mouth down. After another moment, he said, "Do *you* feel like you're worse off?"

I paused, then said, "No. I worry too much, but... really I'm happy most of the time. I like where I am in life. I feel *lucky* to be where I am in life." Another sparring match was beginning in the ring, two men dancing together closely, hunched and wary, occasionally exploding into short volleys of quick punches. A round of encouraging shouts, scattered applause, went up from the onlooking men. I watched, fascinated and detached, as the men circled and circled, their bodies tense and expectant, gloved fists hovering before their faces.

Allan waggled a hand through the air in a dismissive way. "Then don't think about it the way you think other people would think about you. That's some kind of crazy calculus you're trying to do. It doesn't work out. Like, I'm sure you deal with things I can't imagine—although maybe I will soon, if I keep doing things to my knees that make my doctor yell at me. But don't feel like you have to act like your life has all kind of strife in it that it doesn't, just because Roy's does, or did."

I was nodding again. We were both talking circuitously, but it was all touching on things I had been worrying about without being able to quite articulate it to myself. I watched as one of the sparring men—the black guy I'd been watching jump-rope earlier—lunged forward, delivered a series of three incredibly quick blows that had the onlookers cheering. The match ended, and Roy was stepping forward now, putting on a padded helmet of his own, shaking out his shoulders as he bounced from foot to foot on bent knees and grinned, squaring off with the second-biggest guy there.

"Also," Allan said, with a smile in his voice, "don't let Roy get more wrapped up—" he made a furious circling gesture with one hand "—with his own strife than, you know, he really needs to." I grinned, myself. Then he continued, more seriously, "Although you should ask him about high school sometime, if you haven't already."

"Oh!" I said, surprised. "I will." And, "*Thank* you. We— we should all go out for drinks sometime, or something."

He gave me a big grin in response, the weathered channels in his face deepening.

"Is this kind of a hobby for you?" I had to ask then, with a touch of irony.

He gave a short laugh. "I used to think I'd be a novelist, maybe a journalist. Now I'm just a relic with a mouth."

We grinned for another few moments, then fell into silence, and watched Roy fight. Again, as when I'd watched him shadowboxing in the early morning, I was amazed at how *quickly* he could move, the way he seemed to be able to float his big body through space. Again I became aware of everything that was small, awry, off-kilter about my body. But this time, it just seemed like a fact, the way I preferred it to—not a failure.

Later, when Roy escorted me out, breathing fast, still smiling ear to ear, he asked, "So, what'd you think?"

I said, "I'll be honest, I don't know how much of what you were doing really sunk in that time. But you're right: Allan is *really* good at explaining things."

12

Light in the Forest

It was mid-November, an overcast Saturday, though not too cold. Eduardo and I were finishing up a job for a client, replacing a few beds of mums and late pansies with dwarf yews. It was easy, systematic work, spading up the clumps of flowers—personally I thought they'd been planted too shallowly, though now it only made my job easier—and pulling out the conical little evergreens from their flimsy plastic pots to dig in instead. My head stayed restfully thoughtless as the pair of us bent and dug. Sweat ran down my neck into my t-shirt, pleasantly icy when the wind ran over it, and the mound of discarded flowers in the wheelbarrow behind us grew. The pansies were still blooming, though straggly, and I thought I might rescue one to repot for Asher, along with a yew that wasn't fit to be planted.

As we neared the end of the last bed, the client, Mrs. Petersen, came out on her front doorstep to watch. She was thin, blonde, in her late twenties, and slightly pregnant. I guess "a few months in" was the phrase for it. She had on an oversized hoodie—I wondered vaguely if it was her husband's—and leggings. There were purplish shadows under her eyes, and the corners of her mouth seemed naturally downturning. She said nothing after an initial exchange of hellos, and as Eduardo and I continued, I became uncomfortably aware of the intensity of her gaze.

After spading mulch over the base of a freshly planted yew, I stood up and paused to look at her. She was definitely watching us, both of us. Eduardo was a couple years younger than me, a Guatemalan immigrant, compact, wiry, with very black hair and intensely angled eyebrows over a small, serious face. He didn't talk much, in English or in Spanish, which was of course fine by me—but his wife had recently had twins, and lately he began and ended every job we had together by showing me pictures of them on his phone. Kids I didn't really get; but seeing him so happy, thumbing through snapshot after snapshot of his plump, shyly smiling wife with the two flush-faced bundles, made me happy.

Both of us had warmed up enough to have stripped down to t-shirts. As I looked at Mrs. Petersen, she made no effort to hide the fact that she was looking us over methodically: arms, chests, the arch of Eduardo's back as he dug his spade in. Briefly she made eye contact with me, then resumed gazing without a change of facial expression. I shook my head slightly and returned to my work.

Fifteen minutes later, as I was reaching for the bills she'd counted out for us, she paused to extend one hand and clasp it around mine. "Thank you," she said with unnecessary fervor. Her facial expression still hadn't changed. I removed my hand without saying anything, and waited for the money.

Finally she looked slightly disappointed, turning her face down and to one side.

As I checked that I'd loaded everything into my pick-up's bed—I was taking the spent flowers, plus the yew that I'd claimed for Asher—Eduardo made a rare unnecessary comment: "*Es bonita.* Pretty lady." And then he laughed, briefly, at the look on my face.

"Here," he said instead, and handed me his phone, with the latest round of baby photos. I accepted gratefully.

The interaction with Mrs. Petersen had made me uneasy, but it faded as I got on the road. On my way out, I'd texted Asher: "Are you home?"

"Yup!" came the answer, almost immediately. Elated, I stuffed my phone away into my pocket, where it buzzed a few more times. I didn't bother to check, because my mind was already with him.

During the drive over, my mind flickered back a couple more times to Mrs. Petersen, but finally I had to shake my head again. Definitely not my problem. One or two of the guys we worked with might have been game to try something, but with Eduardo and me she was barking up multiple wrong trees.

At Asher's apartment, I hopped out, and then remembered to grab the yew, which had been allowed to grow two trunks, one of them stretching out gracefully to one side. I thought it looked nice, like a bonsai, but it would have been out of place in a uniform suburban bed. I brushed loose dirt off the sides of the pot, popped it under one arm, and then went to ring Asher's doorbell, already rocking up onto my toes in anticipation.

Inside, I could hear a murmur of surprise, but didn't have time to think about it before the door opened, showing me Asher, slightly open-mouthed and wide-eyed. Behind him, seated at the kitchen table were an older woman and man. Both had curling hair, near-black brown heavily mixed with grey. The woman was small, with large dark eyes, wispy grey upturned eyebrows, and large-framed glasses. She perched on the edge of her seat with a quizzical smile on her face. The man was tall, thin, and stooping, with long black brows and a long, finely chiseled nose.

Belatedly, I heard Asher's voice in my head, from two days ago: *And this weekend I'm having my parents over for lunch.*

Slowly I settled square onto my feet. I let out a breath. I became very conscious of the fact that I was wearing a sweat-stained, colorless t-shirt, faded jeans with dirt and paint stains on the knees, and crusted boots. And I had a crooked potted tree under one arm.

"Hi Roy," Asher said, his eyes anxiously tracking whatever was happening on my face, "these are my parents, Rebekah and Orr."

I thought about the texts that Asher had sent me that I hadn't bothered looking at before driving over.

I could feel my jaw and tongue, even my throat, locking up.

What I would really liked to have done then would have been to say, cheerfully, "Hi, it's so nice to see you. I apologize for interrupting your lunch. Asher told me you'd be here, but I totally forgot. I'm really not presentable, so let me let you get on with your afternoon. I'd love to meet you another time." And then I'd get into my truck and drive away.

Instead I just took a step back from the door, and said nothing. My heart pounded.

After a moment, Asher's mother—Rebekah—said, "Roy! We've heard so much about you. Please, you're not interrupting—we were only just getting started. Won't you come in?" Her voice was so kind.

"Yes, come in!" Asher echoed desperately, but his face said he didn't know if he didn't wanted me to stay or go; I hoped it was for my sake.

I held up one finger, and then pointed at my filthy boots with the other hand. Asher nodded. "Oh, yes, thank you, sure," he said, almost babbling.

I stepped back and closed the door again so I didn't keep letting cold air in. Slowly I bent to set down the yew on the welcome mat, and then unlaced and pulled my heavy boots off as quickly as I could. I straightened up, wiped my hands on my jeans (achieving nothing) and then took a deep breath, and another one. Again, I considered getting in my truck and leaving.

I opened the door and stepped inside.

Asher had rolled back into the kitchen to pull out the third chair for me; his legs were kicking restlessly, and I saw him wince and press down on one briefly. I advanced, quickly touched the back of one hand (marginally less dirty than the palm) to his shoulder. I didn't know which of us I was trying to reassure more. And then I ducked my head and extended my hand first to Asher's mother, then to Asher's father. In silence we shook hands. I forced myself to meet their eyes: his mother looked brightly curious, her head cocked to the side slightly; his father just looked mild, patient. I realized that I had no idea what Asher had told them about me.

"Do you want to...?" Asher nodded his chin in the direction of the bathroom. I nodded quickly, grateful, and ducked out to wash my hands and face.

When I emerged, they had resumed chatting and eating. I seated myself gingerly. They all smiled; Asher's smile had recovered some of what I now saw as his habitual mischievousness, though I could still hear his legs kicking against his chair. He slid an empty plate to me. The food looked and smelled good: some kind of grain salad with parsley and tomatoes chopped small, spiced chicken, orange slices, fresh bread. I wondered who had made the food, and then, again belatedly, Asher's voice filtered back into my head, explaining his weekend lunches with his parents: *We swap off places, and whoever hosts does the cooking, too...*

Slowly, I relaxed, just watching and listening. After a minute I felt settled enough to reach for food. Asher's mother had been telling a story about one of her students; she was a high school art teacher, I remembered.

"We just started projects in color," she was saying, in her light, raspy voice, "and he's been doing the most remarkable paintings. They're winter landscapes, that kind of grey-white sky, like just after snow—black trees, snow on the ground. It's all very nicely handled, nice and loose." She made a vigorous sweeping gesture with one hand to illustrate. "But the interesting thing is the light. He's done the light so that it's kind of *splintered*."

Asher made a quizzical expression. I chewed my chicken.

"Oh, you know, like a prism? The light coming down through the trees is splintered into all these different little spears of light, lots of pastel colors—not literal rainbows. And some splinters of black, too."

"Black light?" Asher said.

"Yes, you wouldn't think it would work, but it does. It was the sort of thing where I looked at it and thought, *well, why hadn't I thought of it that way before?* And isn't that just how a winter wood should look."

Asher and his father had the same smile, I thought, a little higher on the left side than the right.

"So I asked him about it, I was just so curious how he was thinking about it. And he didn't seem to want to talk about it, so I left him to it. But later on in class he pulled me aside, and he told me that, in fact, he was mostly blind in one eye, and that's just how the light looks to him sometimes."

"Huh!" said Asher and his father, almost at the same time.

"Yes, imagine that. I had to catch myself before I told him how much of a *pain* depth perception can be when you're drawing, and how there are plenty of painters who might actually appreciate being in his position. I didn't want to come on too strong, you know," she said, with a look of dismay at her imagined forwardness.

"Didn't Dad once tell you he'd get you an eyepatch if he caught you squinting one-eyed at your paintings again?" Asher asked, screwing up one eye demonstratively.

"*Once*? He wore out the tire treads on that one."

"Sexy pirate? Isn't that a thing?" Mr. Klein suggested, but he looked so embarrassed to even be making the joke that Asher and Mrs. Klein burst out laughing at him.

I looked back and forth among the three of them. *Asher-people*, the thought came into my head. It was so easy to see where Asher had come from, his patience, his bright inquisitiveness, his humor. I couldn't imagine my parents talking about any of this; I couldn't imagine them laughing so easily together over little things.

And they had, all three of them, accepted me so easily, silent in their midst, but not ignored. One or another would occasionally look at me to see if I needed anything, if there was anything I wanted to say (not yet, although I was working up to it), or just to include me in a smile.

I had also belatedly remembered that Asher had told me that some of his friends with disabilities couldn't talk with their own voices, had to use tablets or other devices to speak for them—I would have liked to see how that worked, figured

I would at some point in the near future, if things kept going the way they did. (*And when did you become a guy who actually got introduced to friends? To* family? said a voice in my head.) So, it stood to reason that his parents would hardly blink if he had a friend who just took a while to talk—even if he did also interrupt lunch while sweaty and filthy. Working through thoughts like this, I was gradually cooling my shame and embarrassment.

Asher moved his hand onto my arm. His mother's smile might have widened a little, but otherwise, his parents didn't react: also a new, previously unthinkable thing for me.

"Roy," Asher said, his look teasing, "is your plant getting hungry on the doormat?"

"My p-plant?" I managed to say after a moment, startled. I set down my fork, and then I remembered the yew. "Oh! Oh, yes. That was g-g-going to be a present for you." His mother's smile widened even further. "No, he's g-good," I said, "he's a puhh... patient little guy." It had taken me a little while to pick up Asher's gentle style of bantering, when we were first getting to know each other, but now it was easy, especially with two other Kleins in the room.

"What did I do to deserve a present?"

I wanted to say, *just being you*, but resisted while his parents were here. I wiped my mouth with my napkin. "He wouldn't have gg-g-gotten any love b-back where he came f-from. I thought he would be h-happier with your other trees." I pointed to the two in the corner.

"Oh, hey, thank you," Asher said, grinning with real pleasure; the fingers of his small hand flexed slowly. "I can't wait to meet him. Neither can my trees."

"Did you come straight from a job?" Asher's mother said. "Asher tells us you work in landscaping." I looked at her gratefully; she was giving me a chance to excuse my muddy arrival.

"Yes, I did," I said. "So, sorry about—" I gestured to encompass my t-shirt and so on. Everyone murmured that it wasn't a problem, and I felt infinitely better.

These people, I thought.

"Everything went well with the job?" said Asher's father.

"Yeah," I said automatically, "it was easy, just ss-switching out s-seasonal plants. Only..." The image of Mrs. Petersen came back into my head, her darkened, unhappy eyes. I paused, unsure if I wanted to talk about this. But the story pushed its way out of me. "There's s-s-something s-strange about the woman we worked for today. She's pregnant, and young, and she has a bb-beautiful house, but she sssss... suh... she seems very sad."

Asher looked at me with a troubled expression; I think he could sense some of what I wasn't saying.

His mother made a sympathetic noise, her eyes soft. "Does it feel strange to know you can't do anything about it?"

I thought about it. "Yes," I realized. I opened my mouth to say more, and then realized I didn't have anything more to say about it, that that was how it made me feel: strange, and helpless. Mrs. Petersen coming on to me did give me a slight sense of the wrongness, the impatient discomfort that I always felt when women took interest in me. But in her case it hardly seemed to have anything to do with me. I, and Eduardo, had just been there. I looked at Mrs. Klein and nodded once, emphatically.

"You've probably seen quite a lot of strange things in your time, working around people's houses," she said, more lightly.

I laughed, shook my head. "T-t... too many." And, only a little haltingly, I was able to get out the story of the time I'd found a "tame" raccoon being kept by a teenager in the rotting toolshed that his mother wanted demolished, which had ended in tears and rabies shots.

Afterwards, I still found myself prickling with occasional waves of nerves—these were Asher's *parents*, they knew that I was *with* their son, had to be sizing me up, asking themselves all kinds of questions about how on earth I made sense as a match to their clean-cut, college-educated son. But, looking at their faces—I seemed to have pulled the story off, they were chuckling incredulously—I felt a sense that I'd performed *enough*.

The word "perform" did sometimes pop into my head when I was with Asher. When it did, I regretted it. But it was hard to escape the sense that as patient as he was, he was always waiting for me to say more than I felt either capable of or interested in saying. Talking was his element, he'd told me so, directly, but to me it was like fire: untrustworthy, unreliable. I wasn't sure how often I'd imagined a look of disappointed expectation in his eyes when I'd said what felt, to me, like enough, a complete thought—but maybe only left him with more unanswered questions. For a moment I thought back to our conversation in Crown Hill Park, about my past. Immediately I flinched away again.

You can do better, I thought to myself, with a stab of frustration.

I pulled myself out of the spiral, glanced around the table. Asher's parents were talking softly to each other—it sounded like they were sorting out other weekend plans. Asher gave the appearance of listening to them, while slowly starting to stack the emptied dishes that he could reach. But I could tell he had his eye on me.

When he saw that he had my attention, he leaned towards me. "Doing okay?" he said softly.

I gave him a one-sided smile, and raised my eyebrows questioningly: *I don't know, am I?*

"They like you," he said immediately, and even more softly. And he smiled.

My stomach flipped. I couldn't tell if it was his smile, renewed nerves, or both. I raised my eyebrows again, made an *if you say so* face, and then gently nudged his hand aside from the stacked dishes to make it clear that I'd take charge of the washing-up. He gave me an appreciative look, and turned to listen to his parents' conversation again.

I listened in as I scraped off bits of food, did the rinsing and racking in the dishwasher. They were talking about an event that one of Asher's cousins was holding soon—I didn't totally get what, maybe because it was a Jewish thing. But I wanted to understand their patterns, how they thought about things, what they expected of each other. The last time I'd spent any

time with somebody else's family was probably in—Jesus—
high school, back before I quit the soccer team. I felt like a street
dog trying to remember how to sit, roll over, shake, speak.

I was listening so intently to everything in and around the
conversation that it took me a moment to register that they
had actually asked me a question, had all turned to look at me
expectantly. I shook my head quickly and widened my eyes in
apology.

Asher repeated, "November 18th? What do you think,
Roy?"

I took a pause, a long one. First of all, I still wasn't sure
what I was being invited to, and was embarrassed to ask them
to repeat themselves, again.

Second of all: November 18th—three days away—was the
arraignment date for the three men who had tried to take
Asher's wheelchair in the alleyway. And from the innocent
way that Asher was asking about it, I couldn't tell if he had
genuinely forgotten about it—which I couldn't believe—or
if he was putting on a front because he *still hadn't told his
parents about it.*

Which, the more I thought about it, seemed more and
more likely the case, because I could not believe that parents
like Asher's wouldn't have commented at least once about the
court date.

I opened my mouth, but couldn't say anything. I could
tell that Mrs. Klein was getting ready to say something nice—
probably she just thought that I was being shy again. I moved

my gaze to Asher and raised my eyebrows at him slightly. *Did you...?*

When he couldn't hold my gaze, my stomach sank. Mrs. Klein stopped whatever she was going to say; both of his parents looked back and forth between us curiously as the silence stretched on.

I had no intention of forcing Asher to do anything in front of his parents. And Asher hadn't even planned to attend the arraignment, so for him there was no practical conflict—just the symbolic weight of the date. (Though I sure as hell wanted to see the three standing in front of a judge.) So there was still no reason I couldn't just play this whole thing off as me being awkward.

Except that if the assholes *didn't* all take plea bargains, the case would go to trial, and then Asher would be stuck lying to his parents about the nonexistence of multiple future court dates, stretching out over months, all while his stress went through the roof. I'd tried not to subject Asher to this line of thinking too much, but it was often at the back of my mind.

And now Asher was sitting there with a crushingly clear look of guilt on his face, his legs so tense that they were trembling continuously, hovering a few inches out of the seat of his chair, while his parents continued to look back and forth between us in confusion.

I had to say *something*. Physically, I forced out the words: "I'm really sss... sorry—"

"Oh, no no no," Mrs. Klein rushed to say, leaning forward so quickly that her glasses shifted half an inch down her nose;

distractedly she pushed them back up again. "If it's at all an issue for you, please don't worry about it, it's just a little get-together."

"Actually..." Asher said slowly. I looked back to him, worry twisting through my stomach. He didn't look up at any of us, and I could tell he was holding himself very carefully in his chair, trying to minimize the distraction of his trembling legs. He continued deliberately, "I think... Roy is hesitating because there's something *I* didn't tell you about that date. The 18th."

I crossed one arm across my chest, put my other hand to my jaw to rub it. My heart was pounding, I couldn't escape the sense that I had no idea what was going to happen next—except that Asher had to be feeling twenty times worse than I was right now. I wanted to go to him and hold his hand, but didn't want to distract.

The next time he looked up, I did my best to give him an encouraging smile. He returned it with sudden and astonishing warmth. I blinked in surprise—and Asher took a deep breath, and began to tell his parents the story of how we'd met.

13

Killing Time Till the Day of Execution

I was flat on my back in the alleyway. Cold, damp asphalt pressed into my back, darkness pressed around me, pushing at the edges of my vision. I felt thick, cold, sick. I could hear voices: hard, mocking, incomprehensible. The sounds came in snatches, sudden harsh syllables jabbing into my hearing. Sometimes they floated nearer, as if the men were coming back, and my heart pounded; then they faded off again.

With my good arm I reached for something to help me, feeling around for anything, but all my hand encountered was empty air, and the chill, pebbly asphalt. I couldn't push myself up, I felt so cold and weak, as if pressed into submission by the darkness.

Suddenly the voices blared close and *loud*, as if the men were standing over me in a circle and shouting into my face.

But I could see nothing but darkness. They were shouting and shouting, broken, incomprehensible syllables.

The confusion was so total that I woke up, panting with fear.

I blinked up at the ceiling and ran my hand over the comforter over and over, working to convince myself that I was *here*, not *there*. Under the covers, my legs were kicking frantically, my bad arm was snapping in and out, and my wrist felt excruciatingly tight, the pain bright and urgent. In a way, the pain was nice: it proved that I wasn't in the dream.

As my head slowly cleared, I registered with a sinking sense of regret that Roy wasn't there. He hadn't been able to stay over for several nights. I craved his touch, the sound of his breath, so badly that my chest ached.

My parents had asked me if I wanted to see a therapist, after I had told them about the nightmares, after I had told them about the men in the alleyway. The main reason I had said *no, not yet* was because Roy was so often there, muffling the panic, making me smile. But of course, he couldn't always be there.

I had to breathe, slowly, for what felt like hours before I could fall asleep again.

The next day at work, Francis asked me if I was coming down with something, and I almost said yes, because I felt that miserable.

***

The third time Amy was mean to Roy, I knew I needed to call her out on it. Conveniently, about fifteen minutes later, Roy excused himself from the table to take a client's phone call. As soon as he was out of earshot, I leaned toward Amy, and put my hand on her upper arm. "Amy." We were at a downtown restaurant; she appeared to be distracted by a large party of sorority girls exiting noisily into the night. When the door finally closed behind their clattering heels and stream of bright chatter, we could feel a ghost of the cold air they'd let in.

"Amy!" This time she swung around to look at me, with an expression of mild amusement. The warm lighting filtering down from the shaded pendulum lights overhead was a color that I thought of as particularly "Amy:" a coppery-gold that made her curly hair and pale eyes glow, like a foxy Renaissance angel.

"Hm?"

"Amy, I feel like you're being... snippy to Roy."

For a moment she looked blank, and then a slightly wary look came into her eyes. "What makes you say that?" she said, with careful neutrality.

"It's—I feel like I'm nitpicking." I was already doubting myself, but pressed ahead; I didn't know how soon Roy's call would end. "But it's—something about the way you keep saying *'oh?'* back at him, no matter what he says." I replicated the subtly challenging, contemptuous tone I'd heard, and the slight lift of her left eyebrow that went with it. Afterwards I had to stop myself from smiling nervously, undercutting what I was trying to say.

Amy looked aside a few moments, before lifting one hand to prop her chin on it; with the other she started slowly rubbing the plastic cuffs of her forearm crutches, propped on her side of the table. "Don't apologize," she said a little absently. She returned her gaze to me, looking serious, almost severe. "I honestly don't remember doing that, but you're right that I probably did. Sorry. Mea culpa."

I relaxed a little. I started rubbing my hand over my right hip; both had been uncomfortably tight since the nightmare, which always made me a bit paranoid of having to have hip surgery done again. Worries on worries.

I was so used to Amy that when getting ready to introduce Roy to her, I had forgotten—maybe conveniently—that her high spirits could also come out as prickliness, which I was sometimes exasperated by, and sometimes actually admired. Between the two of us, I was definitely the pushover.

I could tell she was also looking around now to make sure Roy wasn't coming back imminently. At about the same moment, we both located him outside, a few windows down from where we were sitting. He was standing with his back to us, clearly still on the phone. Reflexively I admired the way the column of his neck looked when his head was bent down, the way that his hair came to a point at the nape of his neck, which I liked to kiss when I could.

Amy looked at me again. "I do like him, you know." I almost let out an audible *phew*. "But, like... you know I have insanely high expectations for anybody who expects to be with you." I ducked my head, embarrassed, and she mimicked the gesture back at me, adding a cartoonish "Aw, *shucks*."

"You're not making this easier, Amy!" But I was laughing at her.

"I know, I'm sorry—"

"But fine," I said after we'd composed ourselves, "I appreciate it, you know I do. But go easy on him. You know he's super shy—"

"You *don't* say," she said with rich sarcasm.

"Come on!" I said indignantly. "You're doing it again." It had been painfully obvious that Roy had been intimidated by Amy as soon as the night had started, taken aback by her quick glances and remarks, which was why I had been set on edge by even the very subtle mockery that had seeped into her handling of him.

"Sorry, sorry—" She looked genuinely guilty, her cheeks flushing a bit. She started making a circular gesture with both of her hands. "It's just, you know, I'm used to *our* back-and-forth, I have high expectations for this guy, and he's sweet, it's so clear that he's crazy about you, but he's like..."

"Not what you expected," I finished bluntly; I was trying to steel myself, on Roy's behalf. Again she looked guilty, and glanced out the window at his back. "We talked about this already, Amy."

"I knowwww," she said, swaying side to side in her seat. "It's just—he's such a jock, Asher! It's bizarro!"

"I think you mean 'super hot,'" I corrected her, primly. We were both enjoying letting humor loosen us up again, without leaving honesty out of the question.

"Fine, yes, he is an excellent specimen of the masculine form." She batted her eyelashes at me. "I admit—it's not that I wasn't listening when you told me he was huge and buff and huge, but... *yeah*. It's like my mental picture frame couldn't go that big. Does he like, carry you around your apartment and shit?"

I had to smirk. "Actually, yes. Buff boyfriend versus assistive technology—" I rocked my head from side to side, as if weighing the choice. "Ehhh... not always the *practical* option, but all things considered, I'd say boyfriend wins."

"God!" Amy flung her head back, rolling her eyes. "Where did I go wrong? Vikram won't carry me."

I burst into incredulous laughter. "Is this a *problem* for you?" Inwardly I felt a twinge of happy relief that Vikram was still in the picture; it had felt like Amy'd been avoiding mentioning him for a while.

"Yeah, he says it's demeaning to women—"

"Oh my god, what?"

"Well you know he's all up in arms about resisting his super patriarchal upbringing—also he says I'm 'too long'..."

"Wait, what? Oh, crap, Roy is coming back in. Anyway, can you please work on being less, like, reverse-ableist now?"

"But jocks deseeeerve it, Asher—"

It was nothing we hadn't joked about before, but... "This one is *my* jock."

She reached out and touched my shoulder quickly, her eyes soft. "Yes, I'll be good. Thanks for calling me out."

Grateful, I smiled back at her.

My brain was still working furiously as Roy strode back in and made his way back to our table. What we hadn't had time to get to (*the world doesn't have infinite time for your neuroses, Asher*, I reminded myself sardonically) was just how oddly put-together a puzzle Roy was, which I thought had to account in part for how edgy Amy had gotten.

The truth was that Amy and I both liked things to go *fast*, when it came to conversation; that we liked to talk a lot, and quickly, was a central pillar of our friendship. "I'm used to *our* back-and-forth," she had said. Neither of us had ever directly acknowledged it to each other, because it felt unworthy, but we both knew that it took each of us a very deliberate mental switch, an almost physical resetting of expectations, to engage with disabled friends who were low-verbal or nonverbal. Slow down, chill out, wait and listen. With each other, there was a guilt-tinged relief in getting to go as damn fast as we pleased, while still enjoying the comfort of not having to explain any disability stuff.

Roy, on the other hand, was a weird inversion: able-bodied as hell, the picture of red-blooded American masculinity (minus the gay part), but *also* close to nonverbal, under the wrong circumstances. I had a pretty firm sense that that uneasy, paradigm-breaking combination was why Amy hadn't been able to stop herself from needling him. And while Roy's difficulties with his stammer made me feel incredibly tender towards him, it would have been a lie to say I didn't, sometimes, feel impatient.

I had worried intensely and often about us being completely mismatched: why the hell would a guy like Roy want to date a guy who couldn't run, hike, climb, or really do anything other than *sit*? But as time rolled on, I was starting to have the sense that all of these weird asymmetries created a kind of momentum in our relationship—the sense that we would be able to keep finding each other interesting for a very, very long time.

Roy pretty perfectly put an end to my frantic train of thought by running his hand along the back of my neck as he walked around me and back to his seat. I smiled up at him, probably fatuously, and he smiled back. And out of the corner of my eye I saw Amy quirk half a smile, too.

The rest of the dinner went great, to my immense relief. I could even feel some of the tension ease out of my legs, so I felt like I was actually sitting in my wheelchair instead of balancing precariously. Amy's veiled needling disappeared, replaced by the tenderly serious attitude she took on when she was really listening to someone, and Roy even relaxed enough to make her laugh with a quietly mischievous remark. I knew that would be a big step forward for him in her mind, compared to the tense, awkward, almost flinching Roy she'd seen at the beginning of the evening. When that happened, I gave her a challenging little smile: *See? He is fun.* And she gave me back a chastened grin.

Afterwards, we shared an accessible cab back to Amy's and my apartment block, and it was *fun*, incredibly so. All riding along together in the dark, the streetlights sliding by outside, Roy holding my hand… The night took on a giddy, loose quality, especially when Roy cracked one of the windows to dilute the oppressive odor of pine car freshener, and chilly air began streaming in. It felt like we laughed the whole way home.

On the sidewalk outside our apartments, Amy surprised Roy by lifting up her crutches to give him a big, long hug, squeezing him around his middle; I ducked my head and grinned at how big his eyes got. Then she crutched over to bend and give me a hug of similar duration, finishing it off with a peck on my cheek. "G'night, babe."

"G'night, Amy. And thanks." We exchanged a last smile before she waved and turned off towards her apartment.

Inside my kitchen, Roy shut the door behind us; while I was looking around, letting out a long breath, I heard him make a distinctly *animal* sound behind me, and then his boot steps came at me swiftly, and his arms wrapped around me from behind. "Whoa! Hi!"

"Mmmm—" As I laughed helplessly, he kissed his way up and down my neck, nipped at my ears, slid his heavy hands up my chest and face to run fingers through my hair, then back down again to unbuckle my seatbelt.

"Oh, *hi*—" Now he was sliding his hands down my back, gently pressed his fingers against the backs of my hips and down to my ass.

"Ready?" he asked softly.

"Yes—I think—" I thought I knew what he was asking, and then he did shift to one side, slid one arm behind my shoulders and one under my knees, and picked me up smoothly and swiftly.

Now we were face-to-face, something I otherwise never got to experience when the other person was standing. I looked deeply into his eyes and smiled, my heart pounding with happy excitement. "Hi," I said again.

"Hi," he said this time. His smile made my stomach feel like jelly. I kissed him for a long time, feeling light and easy and safe in his arms.

When we broke, he cocked his head in the direction of the bedroom. "Shall we...?" I grinned and nodded, and he strode off.

"Amy's jealous that you carry me around, 'cause her man won't," I murmured teasingly in his ear. He snorted. "I got the best one..." I said in a sing-song, and kissed his neck slowly. He made another animal sound, flipped off the kitchen lights with his lower hand, and we passed into the bedroom in darkness.

***

Again I'm in the alleyway. This time I'm in a chair, not mine: a shitty metal chair, like in a movie interrogation scene, and they fan out around me like movie interrogators. I feel profoundly homeless, in alien territory. Again I can't understand their voices. They gabble harsh, excited sentences that echo off of the brick walls enclosing us. Now there's no alleyway, just a little box of brick with the dark figures circling me around; it's not clear whether they're figures, or shadows on the walls.

I'm struggling to move, kicking my legs, struggling to straighten my contracted arm. I don't know what I'll achieve, but there's a sense that rocking, knocking over the chair will break the spell, the dream.

After another interval of distorted time, the alien voices echoing in my ears, I realize what the issue is. They've tied down my good arm, my only arm, to the arm of the shitty metal chair. When I realize that, that I have nothing, the fear is so profound that I want to sink down and black out, let it all collapse on me so I don't have to feel anything anymore.

I wake up, and this time Roy is there. He holds me while I cry.

14

All Rise

We both woke up early in the morning, not much after sunrise, despite the fractured night—or maybe because of it. Unusually, Roy looked tired, with a heaviness to his eyes, but he looked at me alertly. Neither of us said anything, but we each moved to touch the other. I reached out my arm to him, ran the pad of my thumb over his brows. He rolled onto his side, rested his top hand against the side of my face, and closed his eyes with contentment as I stroked, pushing away the tension that I knew he tended to store there.

I marveled at him, at his nearness and realness: another man, here in my bed, a man who let me touch him and love him.

After a little while, he opened his eyes again and nudged my hand away with his face, smiling affectionately: *My turn*, his eyes said.

He moved his hand to my bad arm and started stroking from the shoulder down. I sighed as his blunt fingers dug into the perpetually tense muscle of my upper arm, then slid down to pull gently and steadily against the contracted elbow joint, releasing tension in my wrist.

I closed my eyes. Maybe I could fall asleep again. I had well over an hour until I needed to start getting ready for the day. Roy's hand released my arm, slid down to my hand. There was a brief break in contact, and then suddenly his fingers were stroking the underside of my contracted hand. Without thinking about it, I jerked away, opening my eyes.

There was a crease between Roy's brows again, and he looked at me questioningly.

"Oh! Sorry," I said. A wave of fatigue hit me then, mixed with the twist of anxiety that had followed me up from out of my nightmares. I felt heavy, sour.

I turned my face away from Roy a little and had to think. "It's just... still a weird spot for me. I don't get touched there that often."

I looked back at him again, smiled and tried to put some humor into my voice. "It's like, I dunno, your armpit or something."

Roy didn't say anything, just kept looking at me with those worried brows and heavy eyes. And suddenly, for the first time since we had started seeing each other, I felt a stab of wholly irrational annoyance with him. That solidity of presence, those expectant eyes seemed suddenly oppressive: an unfamiliar object in my space, distracting at best, alien at worst.

It was such a small thing. But Roy saw that moment in me, felt it; I knew he did. And I saw him withdraw into himself, in turn. It was if shutters went down behind his eyes. He looked blanker, flatter. I had seen this happen to him, but I had never been the cause before.

On some level I knew that I would soon enough be horrified that I had felt that way. It was perverse, ungrateful. But in the moment, all I could feel was tired.

I was tired of waking up crying and spasming, and needing to be comforted. I was tired of being evasive with Amy, other friends, coworkers—making up deadlines or illnesses when I was really just uneasy and underslept. I was tired of worrying about the arraignment, tired of dreading the next call from the police station or the district attorney's office.

And I was beginning to become aware that the pain in my lower back that always came with restless nights was accompanied this time by the creeping burning and numbness that threatened the onset of a pinched nerve. And that might take weeks to resolve, given that I did nothing but put pressure on my lower back. And the whole time I'd be worrying that it meant that my scoliosis was worsening.

I was tired of the *sensation* of fear. The constancy of it, the shame. In the mornings, I pushed it down into a hard knot in my stomach so I could talk, work, travel; by the evening it had unraveled itself again, welled up to consume my nights. It was getting so bad that even when I was chatting with my parents or Amy, I sometimes felt as if I were simply looking for a distraction. Anything to fill up time when I'd otherwise have to think my own thoughts.

It all seemed simultaneously so petty and so crushing. I wished I could just close my eyes and snap back instantly into the blankness of sleep.

Nothing really happened in the alleyway.

Nobody hurt you.

I had been trying to convince myself of that for weeks; it still wasn't working.

By this point, Roy and I had been staring at each other wordlessly for so long that I had lost any sense of what the look on his face might mean. I became aware that I hadn't been able to draw a full breath for some time. I forced myself to exhale hard, blowing it out through my mouth. Now I became aware that Roy was moving his jaw and blinking in a way that meant he wanted to say something, but was having trouble.

This, at last, roused something in me, a flicker of the familiar tenderness. But still I couldn't manage to do anything about it.

Finally Roy ended it by simply rolling to the other side and getting out of bed. Silently, he padded around the bed and toward the bathroom, rubbing the back of his head slowly, his face tilted away from me. I retained enough decency not to pretend to go back to sleep. Instead I stared up at the ceiling until I could hear the shower start in the bathroom.

Somehow that simple release of sound seemed to break the spell, the alien stasis that had fallen on me. I reached out my good arm to grab Roy's pillow, flung it across my face and pushed it down until I could shout into it: "*Fuck!*"

And then, more softly: "Coward."

I flung the pillow aside again, and then roughly pushed myself up to sitting, disregarding the flare of pain along my spine. I flung back the covers, pressed the heel of my hand against my mouth, and stared down at my legs as if they told the truth of the situation: bent, emaciated, immobile.

I sat like that for some minutes. Thoughts went through my head furiously, but I don't know if I could have named any of them. I heard the water shut off again in the shower.

I twisted to reach my cellphone on the nightstand; I set it against one thigh and feverishly tapped out an email. The uncomfortable prickling warmth and occasional metallic stabs of nerve pain ran up and down my spine.

Hi everyone, I'm feeling under the weather and won't be able to make it into the office today. But I'll still be good to go on the deliverables we discussed last Thursday; please expect to see them by...

I could hear the clink of the loose towel bar as Roy replaced his towel in the bathroom. I hit *send*, and by the time the bathroom door opened, I had begun the careful transfer to my wheelchair. I could hear Roy step out into the hall and pause in the bedroom doorway, but couldn't yet bring myself to look up. For another half a minute, I let myself focus on edging over the transfer board, push by push. I thought in a flat kind of way about the pain in my back and the way that it was beginning to transmit itself to my hips.

I could tell that Roy was still standing in the doorway. As soon as I got seated in my chair, a sigh of relief pushed itself out of my chest. I felt I could think more clearly: for now, the change in posture had relieved the pain in my back, though the tightness in my hips meant that my legs and feet were hovering out of the seat. I put my good hand on my left knee, pressed downward for a long moment, more for the sensation of force than because it would do any good, and then raised my head to look at Roy.

"I'm sorry," I said.

Still silent, he crossed the room swiftly and came to the side of my wheelchair. Gently he wrapped one arm around my shoulders and one around my head, pulling me towards his chest.

It took me a moment to let myself lean into him. "I know you felt it too," I said into his arms, muffled.

As soon as I'd completed the sentence, the words registered, perversely, as a stock phrase from flirty pop songs. My mouth twisted. But Roy only nodded against the top of my head.

"It's going to be okay?" I said, still muffled.

He nodded again, and then slowly released me, stood looking down at me seriously.

I took a breath and said carefully, "I think I'll go with you today."

Roy's mouth opened; his eyes widened.

Because today was, of course, the arraignment. We would find out how the three men in the alleyway would plead to their charges, whether we could expect the swift resolution of a plea bargain, or a trial that would certainly mean weeks, and maybe months, of testimony and argument and delay.

Except that I'd been saying for weeks that I wouldn't go, couldn't stand it, would twiddle away at work as if nothing were going on, until my father and Roy had sent word back. At least I'd had the excuse that my mom, too, had decided that she wasn't up to it.

For the first time that morning, Roy spoke: "Are y-y-y-you s-sure?" His head quested in space slightly as he worked over the repeated syllables; his brows were deeply furrowed, and he had put a hand to his chin.

I put my hand up to hold his forearm. "Yes," I said. "I'm sure. Let's get ready."

***

I dressed carefully, as if armoring myself. Roy, already dressed in a button-up shirt and a pair of dark jeans that were considerably less faded and creased than his typical wardrobe, sat and sometimes watched me, sometimes seemed to be thinking to himself, one hand again to his mouth. He had made coffee for both of us, and the aroma filled the apartment.

With my back and hips acting up, putting on pants was a struggle, and I could see that Roy would have liked to help me as I leaned back and painstakingly inched them up my legs with the help of the grabber stick that extended my reach. But when he looked at me inquiringly, I just gave him a smile to say that I wanted to work on it myself, and he slowly relaxed back into his chair again.

The silence around us was heavy but, thankfully, not oppressive; it just seemed like it would have been too much work for either of us to say anything, that we each needed to be alone with our thoughts.

I was working, in fact, on *not* having any thoughts. I focused on breathing deeply, on calculating each motion and registering the various pains that ran through my body—feeling them all, but letting them go, convincing myself that they would run their course through me, and then away again. This was how it went; this was me.

As I finished up, Roy finally broke the silence to call an accessible cab. Holding hands, we waited.

***

The courtroom was oak-paneled, hushed. When Asher and I rolled in, a handful of people turned at the sound of my steps, the hum of his chair's motor. Several openly stared at him. I could see him tense, his knees drawing up, and I gently pressed a hand into his shoulder.

I picked one person to stare down. When he had dropped his gaze and turned around again, the others followed suit. I could hear Asher exhale, and I gave his shoulder a squeeze.

I scanned the courtroom. The walls above the wood paneling were painted a dull forest green, and the floor was a sad-looking flecked linoleum. I would have loved to pull it up and replace it with something to match the paneling and green paint. There were no windows, but heavy fluorescent lights overhead cast even, bright white light on the dozen or so people scattered around the room. In here, it was impossible to tell what time of day it was.

Seated towards the front of the room, facing us in profile, there was a stern-looking woman: middle-aged, with dark blonde hair, riffling through a stack of files. It was Sylvia Ganon, the deputy district attorney who was leading Asher's case.

When she realized Asher had arrived, she started, and hurriedly squared up her papers before sliding out of her seat to come and greet us. Asher and I exchanged an embarrassed look. Even if we were early enough that the court was still quiet, she had to be busy, and we'd both hoped to arrive without causing any fuss.

She had barely gotten past "I didn't expect to see you here today, Mr. Klein," her thin dark brows raised quizzically, before a small, breathless man in a dark suit and yellow tie hurried over to hover at the edge of our group. I was annoyed by his cringing posture even before he started talking. And then he said to Asher, without really making eye contact, "I'm sorry, sir, but were you planning on—sitting there?"

Asher blinked and looked down and around. We were close to the back of the room, where there were rows of fixed wooden benches clearly intended for members of the public. But we were far enough away from the entry doorway that Asher's chair wouldn't have blocked traffic, or even slowed it down.

"Oh, um," Asher said, his eyes a little wide. "Yes? Around here, if that's okay, sir."

"Oh!" said the man, startled, as if Asher had said something mildly offensive. "No, I'm sorry, I'm afraid that's not okay. That would be obstructing an emergency exit route."

How could someone manage to be so apologetic and such an asshole at the same time? The man glanced in my direction, saw my face, and cringed further, which I guess should have been gratifying. But what would have been *really* gratifying would have been throwing him down the aisle.

Asher gave a long exhale through his nose, looked back towards the entryway, and then up at me, his mouth and eyes tight. His look said, *Please deal with this.* His right hand was clenched against his chest, the knuckles showing painfully through the skin, and I could tell that every movement was still hurting his back.

Luckily for the man in the yellow tie, Ms. Ganon answered before I could. "That's ridiculous," she said, pushing back a loose strand of hair and looking past him in a way that suggested that she was already thinking about something else. "This aisle is obviously wide enough to accommodate... whatever it is you're worried about. Anyway, Mr. Klein is the primary witness in one of today's cases. Let him sit where he wants."

"Oh, but—" the man began, raising his hands and widening his eyes to show the seriousness of the issue.

"Benedict," said Ms. Ganon, still not looking at him, "do you really not have anything better to do right now than undermine the ADA?"

Benedict closed his mouth, dropped his hands, and edged away from the group a few steps before turning on his heel and hurrying away, his shoulders up around his ears.

Asher and I exchanged a look. I forced myself to relax my hands, which I'd been clenching without realizing it. Ms. Ganon, meanwhile, was still staring off, clearly thinking. So her apparent distraction hadn't just been an act—although it was also obvious that she was used to dealing with Benedict. A moment later, her gaze swung to Asher. "So you decided to come," she said, her tone much softer.

"Yes," he said, obviously embarrassed, and was starting to say something apologetic, when she interrupted him in a kind way, "It'll go faster than you expect. Don't worry. And I can almost guarantee you they'll take the plea bargain."

"*Almost*?" Asher said. The fingers of his small hand spasmed.

"Well, you know I don't like making promises." She gave a small smile. "But from my perspective, it would be highly inadvisable for any one of them to decide to make a break for it, so to speak. Bachman especially, since he already has the record." That was the guy who had run out of the alley first; he had a previous charge for disorderly conduct after getting onto a bus drunk and belligerent and trying to pick a fight with a couple of college students.

"Right, right," Asher said hastily, his eyes continuing to search her face for reassurance. I stood and listened as she once again rattled off the details of the plea bargain that she'd worked out. I had the sense that she was going into a kind of professional autopilot, as much for her own benefit as for

Asher's. Meanwhile, Asher shifted uncomfortably in his chair, one corner of his mouth occasionally drawing back with pain.

A few minutes later, Asher's father arrived, as Ms. Ganon was concluding with, "Anyway, we can at least be happy that the office agreed that the idea of bringing charges against *Roy* was ridiculous—"

"Oh, please!" Asher exclaimed—I was glad to see that indignation brought some color back into his face. Then he started in surprise as his father stepped up behind him and laid a hand on his shoulder in greeting. "Oh, Dad, hi—"

"Good morning," Mr. Klein said, with an inquiring look. "What's ridiculous?"

"Oh, we're back on the idea that Roy went beyond 'defense of another,' the way that he went after those guys..." Now it was my own turn to shift uncomfortably, especially since, unfortunately, this wasn't the first time that I'd ended up in the dicey territory at the edges of self-defense/defense of another. Though I hadn't admitted it to Asher.

"Oh, well now," Mr. Klein said, in a way that suggested that the question was too ridiculous to even bear thinking about. It was comforting.

Ms. Ganon, meanwhile, had been drawn slightly to one side by a younger woman in a dark suit, and was listening intently as the woman murmured rapidly in her ear. A few moments later, she said a distracted good-bye to all of us as she allowed herself to be drawn away and back up the aisle toward the front of the room. The energy level in the room was ramping up—more legal-looking people were pacing in and out, or conferring in front of the judge's seat.

"Good morning, Dad," Asher said, more formally.

"You made it," was all Mr. Klein said, with his usual fond smile. "Roy—" He extended his hand for me to shake, as I nodded a greeting.

We moved to get seated so we could finally clear out of the aisle (other than Asher; screw Benedict). Concealing my regret, I let Mr. Klein take the outermost seat so that he could sit next to Asher, and let my mind drift as they bent their heads together to talk quietly. Mr. Klein rested his hand against the back of Asher's upper arm. I twisted sideways a little so that I could lean an arm on the back of the bench and watch the courtroom fill up. Occasionally I tuned in to the sensation of my heart speeding up with a kind of expectant, eager anger. As much as it terrified Asher, paralyzed him, I *wanted* the confrontation that today would bring.

It was during one of those upswings of adrenaline that I saw the door open to admit William Riley: the last man of the three in the alleyway to leave his hands on Asher, the man whose wallet I had taken. I tensed, leaned forward. I remembered the sight of him awkwardly gripping Asher as he started to slide out of his chair—one hand pulling back at his shoulder, the other hooked under his armpit. I thought about how at least one of the three men must have thought to undo Asher's seatbelt, laughed and held back his good arm when he panicked and protested. Maybe it had been Riley. I felt the blood run hot inside me. Riley turned and saw me, and froze. I heard a rushing in my ears.

I saw another familiar face appear past Riley's shoulder. Bachman: his look hardened when he saw me, even as Riley dropped his face and started to walk fast up the aisle.

I held Bachman's gaze for another moment, pushing hard; he tilted his head back challengingly. I ground my knuckles into the back of the bench until the pain went from dull to sharp. Then I forced myself to take a deep breath, breaking off the eye contact. I leaned forward to touch Asher's shoulder in warning. He started at the touch, glancing at me. He must have known what the look on my face meant because a look of purest panic came over him.

I felt a furious regret, then, that I had let him come. What was the point?

Just as Riley drew level with him, Asher's eyes flicked towards the aisle, and his whole body went into spasm, first flinging him back against his chair as his legs suddenly thrust out against his footplates, and then pulling him inward on himself as everything contracted again. I could hear him gasp. Around the courtroom, heads turned to look. I wished I could physically force them away again. Mr. Klein was leaning protectively around him and holding his white-knuckled left hand, saying something softly into his ear. Asher hunched, breathing hard, as his legs continued jerking under him, his back twisting awkwardly to one side.

At least Riley kept his face averted as he hurried by. At least Bachman only seemed to want to look at me, until finally a man, their lawyer, came to collect them, stowed them away in seats at the front of the room. Where was the last one, the third man?

A middle-aged woman had followed them into the court-room. She had the same hollow cheekbones and sandy hair as Riley. A sister? I saw her give Asher a furtive glance before hurriedly sliding into a bench on the other side of the aisle, several rows forward. I couldn't read her facial expression, but her shoulders were hunched, defensive.

I saw all of this in flashes, everything seeming so fast, so flashbulb-vivid, that it was as if I saw each motion flick by twice. This happened to me sometimes when I was fighting: my brain felt physically hot, overstimulated and yet craving more. I saw Ms. Ganon looking back, her dark brows pinched together; I saw all the people continuing to stare at Asher. I looked at the backs of two of the men who had attacked Asher —there was no other word for it, even if he hadn't been hurt— and watched as they shifted their shoulders, leaned to consult with the lawyer, raised a hand to scratch an ear, seemed to stiffly restrain themselves from looking back at us. Every motion of theirs, no matter how slight, seemed magnified in my vision.

Asher was finally raising himself, pushing up against his armrest. I felt strangely far away from him. I leaned my elbows forward onto my knees, stared down as I rubbed the knuckles of my left hand into my open right hand over and over. I had to calm down. Our case wouldn't even be the first one to be called today.

I forced myself to breathe deeply. With regret, I felt the heat of anger seep away, leaving me feeling smaller, duller.

When I looked up again, there was one more man sitting alongside Riley and Bachman.

They're just men, I told myself. There was no meaning in the sight of them, the three of them; for now, I had to believe that.

To my right, Mr. Klein was sitting very upright, his mouth set, his hand still on Asher's armrest. From the aisle, Asher glanced at me, still pale, with one knee lifted unnaturally high, but he managed a wry look—something along the lines of, *What have we gotten ourselves into?* I managed to smile back at him.

I wished we weren't so far away from each other.

We waited. None of the three of us bothered to make conversation. Time seemed to telescope in and out.

Fifteen minutes later, fifty minutes later, the judge arrived. I shook myself out of my daze. She was a surprisingly small woman with short-cropped, grey-brown hair, pointed features, and glasses. We rose as instructed when she was announced. (*Except for Asher*, I thought uncomfortably, wondering what it was like to be left out of these rituals.) We sat when she sat. Despite her size, she had a commanding look, glancing around the courtroom sharply as she arranged herself. As she called the court to order in a crisp, carrying voice, I found myself thinking that Asher probably liked her.

A clerk asked Ms. Ganon to approach the podium and identify herself for the record, initiate the hearing for the first case of the day. I leaned back against the bench until I managed to find an angle that let me watch Asher without too much effort, crossed my arms, and got ready to wait again.

There was one case before ours: a disheveled, defiant-looking young woman, fierce-eyed, who was charged with breaking and entering. We watched as she pled *not guilty*, shooting another fierce look back over her shoulder at the rest of the courtroom, as if daring someone to tell her otherwise. I half-listened as the judge rattled through bail arrangements and court dates. My gaze was being drawn again and again to the heads of the three men sitting at the front of the courtroom.

The young woman disappeared, escorted out. My imagination got so heated again that, by the time that Bachman was actually called to the podium—flanked by both Ms. Ganon and his own lawyer—I almost missed it. My pulse thudded as my attention snapped to him. I imagined that I could see a tremor of nervous tension run up and down his arms, which he held stiffly behind his back, one hand tightly gripping the other, fisted hand. Could I see the tendons flexing in his wrists? I could hardly hear what was going on—until I heard, "I plead guilty."

Had I heard right? I instantly looked to Asher and Mr. Klein, and saw Asher closing his eyes and tilting his head back as Mr. Klein leaned to put an arm around his shoulders. Was it relief or anguish? I was bewildered, until I heard the judge go on, "All right. In that case, I'm going to move us on to a longer process where we'll confirm that 'guilty' is the plea that you really want to enter. Will the Deputy Clerk please place Mr. Bachman under oath?"

Suddenly things seemed to snap back into their normal frame. I resisted the urge to shake my head. Asher—how was he? He was leaning to give me another weak smile. Again I returned it. My face felt stiff.

From there, the judge unspooled an infuriatingly long series of questions. *Have you discussed this case completely with your attorney? Is this in fact your own decision to plead guilty? Do you understand the constitutional rights you have given up?* Bachman managed to make all of his "yes" answers sound like disagreement. I wanted to stand up and shout: *What is the point of all of this?*

You should have just taken him away when he said guilty.

It went on. There was a moment when I managed to entertain myself by imagining Asher scolding me for not respecting legal process. But then it hit me for the first time that *if we were lucky,* we'd flush Bachman out of our systems, only to have to do the whole thing over again—and then again. Three men. If Asher didn't melt down by the end of it, I might.

Conscious of Mr. Klein sitting very alert and upright at my side, conscious of Asher's silent suffering as his body reacted with increasing frequency to the exchange before us, I managed to stay coherent for the rest of that long, long morning, excruciatingly suspended between boredom and fury. Bachman was released on bail. The next man took his place at the podium, and then the next.

There were moments when I admired Ms. Ganon's solidity: the whole time, she looked as cool and focused, as unmoved as she had when we'd begun. I wanted to get up and pace around. As the questions went on, I imagined driving my fists into a punching bag over and over again, feeling each impact reverberate up my arms.

I imagined another version of the day, one where Asher and I had just stayed in bed the whole time. I'd wrap my arms around him.

"Well," said the judge finally. She sat up straighter, surveying the courtroom, shoulders back, lips slightly pursed, as if looking for her next target. "Thank you all. We'll adjourn proceedings for lunch now." And she pushed back in her seat.

I rocked back, startled. Three guilty pleas. We had been released. It had been almost three hours since we'd begun.

Mr. Klein was already moving to stand, which made me realize that Asher had already turned his wheelchair and was even further ahead, almost out of the courtroom. Amazingly, the man holding the door for him as he left was Benedict, the ass. As I drew level with him, he avoided my gaze, looking down. I let him stew, moved off without a word. I made it out the front lobby in time to see Asher rolling off the end of the wheelchair ramp to the parking lot. I jogged down the steps, pulling ahead of Mr. Klein, and came down to see Asher just sitting there at the edge of the lot, his face turned up to the late-autumn sunlight, his eyes closed. His small hand was pressed tightly against his chest, and his back was so contracted that he was leaning over his right armrest. But he was taking in the sun and drawing deep breaths—shaky, but slow. I could see his chest shuddering as he exhaled. His eyelashes looked very dark against his cheeks. Mr. Klein and I gave each other a look, slowed, and stood back from him.

Suddenly I felt a hand on my arm, not Mr. Klein's. I shrugged it off with instant annoyance. "Excuse me," said a woman's voice, almost in a whisper. I looked back. It was the sandy-haired woman, the one who looked like Riley. Her hand was still upraised, and she looked up at me with an anxious expression. I folded my arms and looked back at her. Finally it was Mr. Klein who had to say, "Can we help you?"

"I'm—I'm just—" she began. She tried again, darting a look in Asher's direction: "Is he the one who—you know? They did...?"

This time we both just looked at her.

"I just wanted to say—I'm sorry," she said, fumbling, her eyes darting. "I'm—Will Riley, I'm his sister, and we've always had... well, I've had to look out for him a lot, but just, we never imagined—"

"That's very kind," Mr. Klein said after another moment. His face was hard to read, but the woman ducked her head with something like gratitude, and turned to hurry away toward the parking lot. Mr. Klein and I gave each other another look, before turning back to Asher.

He opened his eyes. "Can you take me home?" he said, to both of us. The wind dragged leaves across the pavement, lifted the hair on his forehead.

"Gladly," said Mr. Klein.

15

A Black Door

"It was a little weird... No, not *too* weird, obviously she meant well, and I could tell she wasn't a hundred percent sure she should be saying anything about it to me, anyway. But I think it had been bothering her that she hadn't said something about it before... Yeah, it was maybe a little maternal. No, I *didn't* tell her I already have a mom, Mom."

Asher moved the phone away from his face to give me a disapproving grimace. I was laughing silently at him from where I lay on his living room floor. It was the Sunday after the arraignment, the first day we'd gotten to ourselves since then—until his mom had called.

Asher tilted his face back to the phone. "It's really okay. I am *more* than prepared to forget about it. Yes, I'd rather forget about everything else, too... No. No, I haven't. Mom, I told you yesterday, I'll figure it out. I will. I promise... Okay, you too. I love you. Bye."

He tapped his thumb to the screen to hang up, and then dropped the phone into his lap, exhaling. "Oy vey. Layers on layers."

I gave him a questioning look.

"Yeah, basically as expected. Dad couldn't help telling her about the call that Ms. Ganon made, and Mom must have been pretty wound up about everything still because she got sort of offended about it. Normally I don't think it would even have occurred to her to act that way."

"Offended?"

"Like, annoyed at the implication that my own family wasn't already doing enough to protect me, or get me to advocate for myself, whatever. And annoyed that anyone was trying to take up more of my time over this."

"Ah." I got both types of annoyance.

The day after the arraignment, Ms. Ganon had called Asher unexpectedly, while he was at work. He'd immediately feared the worst—that the men had somehow gone back on their guilty pleas. But after hurried reassurances, it had turned out that she'd really just wanted, in a strange way, to scold him. "To be a better citizen in general, or more of a disability advocate in particular, ideally both," was how Asher had summed it up to me when I had checked in on him that night.

"Obviously," he said now, working his left hand through his hair in exasperation, the fingers of his other hand slowly curling and uncurling, "everyone agrees that I should have called the police earlier. But I'm still not totally sure what she wants me to do *now*. Go chasing after a personal injury case to really make a point? Get the local paper to write an article about it all, so the people who read it can pat themselves on the back for not being terrible enough to try to steal someone's wheelchair?" He made a face. "Awful."

I was probably making the same face. "Weird way to g-g-get on someone's case."

"Yeah, I don't get it. She was so cool every other time we talked with her."

I stretched my arms up so I could rest my head on them. I was wondering how often Asher's disability made people not know where to draw the line when it came to being protective. I repressed a grimace at the thought that it had probably made *me* weird that way at least a few times.

After a moment, I offered, "She was a *little* b-bossy."

Asher laughed. "Fair. But in a cool way, most of the time... Oh, well," he concluded, clearly making an effort to end that train of thought. He pressed his hand down on his armrest, leaned to stretch his back first in one direction, and then the other.

I sat up, crawled to where I could sit and rest my chin on his knees. As he finished stretching, making a satisfied sound, I looked up at him with a "now what?" kind of expression.

He laughed again, and then leaned forward to wrap his arm around my head. I closed my eyes with happiness as he kissed my hair, ran his cool fingers along my neck. "I can't think straight if you're going to look at me that way," he murmured.

"Don't think," I suggested. "Works great for me."

"Very helpful," he said, releasing me, still smiling.

The truth was, I really didn't know what the answer to "now what" might be. Asher's distress during the arraignment had been obvious and intense. Afterwards, his parents had politely made it clear that they wanted to spend as much time as possible alone with him in the following days, so I'd made myself scarce except for phone calls after work, during which Asher was reassuring but vague. I didn't know how his nightmares had been, whether or not he planned to give in to his mother's repeated pleas to find a therapist, or what, really, he thought about the arraignment.

And—it was a silly thing to wonder about, but, not having a real relationship with my parents, I couldn't even imagine what exactly the Kleins managed to fill up so much time together, so many nights in a row. (Part of me couldn't stop worrying, selfishly, about what or how much Asher might have told his parents about me.)

Asher reached forward again to the side of my head, pinched his fingers together to tug my earlobe gently. "You look so worried," he said. "Let's get out of here."

"What do yyy… y-you want to do?"

"Mmm, as little as possible involving thinking. Let's give your prescription a try, Dr. Roy."

I laughed and pressed my face against his legs in a brief hug, before clambering to my feet and heading to grab my jacket.

***

We took the bus downtown, getting off a few stops before the hilly old town district, and setting off with a vague agreement to meander till we hit Charleton, and then go up from there. It was a blustery, fast-changing autumn day. Every minute, the wind seemed to swing around in direction, tearing a succession of thin grey clouds past the sun so that now we were in shade, now we were in sunlight. It was so windy that it was hard to talk without almost shouting, so we just moved, looking at each other to confirm direction anywhere we might want to take a turn, crossing to the sunny side of the street whenever possible. I rested a hand on one of the handles of Asher's wheelchair and let the wind buffet my head empty, enjoying the changing light, the contrast between the air slicing by me and the comfortable warmth I was working up as we made the gradual uphill climb toward Charleton.

Asher had wrapped a scarf around his face almost to the bottom of his nose. (I had to restrain myself from commenting on how cute it was, not wanting to embarrass him about how sensitive he was to cold.) I glanced down every now and then to see the tip of his nose gradually reddening with the chill, his bright eyes darting as he watched all the other people out trying to enjoy the day, pushed around by the wind, scarves and coats flapping. The sidewalks were narrow in the old part of town, so a lot of people had to step aside into the street to get around Asher's wheelchair. But for once, he didn't apologize to everyone, he just nodded to them in thanks. I smiled to myself when I first noticed.

Maybe it was the pleasant physicality of working against the wind, maybe it was just being with each other after what felt like a long separation, but as we neared the intersection where Charleton began, veering off from another street, I started to be conscious that I was feeling warm, anticipatory—aroused. I moved my hand to Asher's shoulder; he looked up me, and his eyes creased with a smile.

We turned onto Charleton, Asher rocking his head from side to side cheerfully in a little celebration of the milestone. A few blocks in, we passed a tiny brick-paved courtyard, fronting a restaurant that hadn't yet opened for lunch. The mouth of the courtyard was half-shielded by two large potted boxwoods, dense with small dark glossy leaves. I paused, pressing my hand into Asher's shoulder to draw his attention, and then jerked my head in the direction of the courtyard when he looked at me. I started in, and he followed me, eyebrows raised inquisitively.

As soon as we were behind the boxwoods, I bent over him and pulled his scarf down to reveal his smiling mouth. I cupped his face with my hands and kissed him again and again. He reached up, grabbed on to the front of my coat. It was quieter in the courtyard, sheltered from the wind. When we finally broke, I savored the warm touch of his exhalation. His eyes glinted as they moved over my face, and he left his hand fisted on my coat for another moment before withdrawing it to his armrest. He tilted his head to the side a fraction, challengingly.

I inhaled harshly and dropped one hand to his lap, grasping one of his thin thighs, dragging my hand up until—both of his legs kicked—I was cupping his groin. He leaned forward, and I heard him groan, low in his throat.

There was a space of suspended time where I slowly, slowly moved my hand against him, leaning my other hand on his armrest, both our heads bent and almost touching. Asher gave a long sigh.

But finally, he gently put his hand to my wrist, grasped it until I stilled. We looked at each other, and he smiled regretfully. I pulled one side of my mouth back. "Later," he promised.

This time, I sighed. I kissed his temple, he pulled his scarf back up, and he led the way back onto the sidewalk. Suddenly nervous, I couldn't help glancing back over my shoulder, but the windows of the restaurant were dark and still. There was no one there to see us.

Silent and wind-buffeted again, we continued up the increasingly steep slope of Charleton; Asher leaned forward in his chair. Snatches of other people's shouted conversations and laughter whipped by us. It wasn't until we were almost at Zeke's that I realized that we had long since passed the alleyway where I had first found Asher, the three men. Surely he hadn't forgotten, though. I wondered.

I didn't have to wonder when we reached Zeke's. Asher took his hand off his joystick and reached out to grasp mine. "Is this the place where you were hanging out when...?" he said over the wind.

I stopped alongside him, and nodded, smiling.

His hand tightened on mine. "Can we go in?"

I knew what he meant: Zeke's was already open, since they served breakfast—but the front door had three steps. "Yeah," I said eagerly, "they have a ramp." I had asked idly the last time I had been by, daydreaming of a scenario like this one. "Let me go in—" He nodded, and I hurried to find someone who could help, thinking that Asher had to be pretty cold at this point.

It was quiet enough inside that Teddy, a tall guy in his thirties with prematurely salt-and-pepper hair, could go back right away to grab the metal ramp from a storage closet. He carried it out, we fitted it into place together, and Asher rolled in, yelling his thanks over a particularly violent torrent of wind.

We ordered tea, coffee, hot biscuits with butter. I held Asher's hand under the table as he looked around at the worn, dark wood paneling; the cramped, brass-tapped bar; the dusty assortment of framed newspaper clippings, postcards, and license plates on the walls; the handful of regulars lingering over conversations. "Checks all the boxes," he concluded, smiling, before tugging at his hand to gently free it from mine, moving it to rub his small hand, whose fingers were stiffly bent. "Sorry," he said, "still freezing."

"Should've let me warm you up more," I said.

He choked back a laugh and then cleared his throat loudly —Teddy was coming with the food. I wrapped my hands around my mug and grinned down into my coffee.

We talked lazily: funny little things we'd noticed on the walk over, work, books. (The last time we'd gone to the library together, I'd grabbed a copy of *Catch-22* from a display on our way up to the check-out counter. I'd started to try to read more often, so I could share more with Asher, and I was pleasantly surprised by how much more I liked it when I had him to talk to afterward.) Asher tried to convince me again to join his family's Thanksgiving dinner. I still wasn't sure if I was up to it, really was taken aback by how fast Thanksgiving had come. The arraignment had stood in the way as a glaring distraction.

In fact, this was the first time that day that Asher outright mentioned the arraignment: "So you're willing to sit through a million hours of court for me," he said teasingly, "but not come and eat turkey with a few extra Kleins?" I put my head down, flushing. I wasn't sure whether I was being reluctant to the point of rudeness. At the same time, I hung onto one logical point: as hard as it was to believe in the moment, we had only been seeing each other for just over a month. As little experience as I had with family stuff, I was pretty confident that one month was soon to be showing up at a big family event. Asher's parents *had* invited me themselves to a family event, that first awkward lunch when I'd met them, but it was easy to tell myself that they'd just been trying to be nice.

I could see Asher really wanted me to come, but he didn't push when I said nothing more. He just smiled at me with the same glint in his brown eyes that he'd had in the courtyard where we'd kissed.

The memory of how he'd looked after the courtroom flashed back into my mind then, superimposed: his frightening paleness, his eyes tightened with stress, the slow distortion of his posture by his twisting back. I pushed it away, though I knew we needed to go back to it at some point, and soon. But it was so good to see him smile now.

We ordered more tea, more coffee, and then—just before the lunchtime crowd arrived—burgers. By the time we had picked over the last of our fries, I thought it was reasonable to order a beer. To my surprise, Asher did too. He waggled his eyebrows at my expression as Teddy left, and then cheersed me when our drinks arrived.

We fell into longer and longer periods of comfortable silence, just watching the people at other tables, the passersby still whipped by the wind outside, dry leaves flying by. We held hands across the table. I thought about kissing him in bed, later. The afternoon light mellowed.

As I finished my beer, I was just steeling myself to ask Asher how he felt about the arraignment, when he squeezed my hand and said, "Hey, Roy. Tell me about the first boy you fell in love with."

I rocked back, rolling my head to one side. "Duhhhh... d-d-d... duhh... *damn*." I whacked my free hand into my thigh out of irritation both at getting preempted, and at my stutter.

"What?" Asher seemed to realize that I wasn't reacting to only his question.

"I was jjjj... j-just set to ask you ab... ab-about the arraignment." Asher's contracted arm tightened jerkily across his chest, and he glanced away briefly, an uncomfortable half-smile on his face. "Guess you win at hard q-questions," I continued.

He squeezed my hand again. "I won't forget yours is queued. Couldn't forget, really."

"I figured. Ffffff... okay. Damn. D-do I really have to do this?"

"It would make me happy," he suggested hopefully.

"Even if it's not a happy ssss... suh... s-story? And I t-take forever?"

"Does it have to do with high school?" Asher said, un-expectedly. I looked at him, taken aback. He said, "Could have been a lucky guess—or an obvious one. But no—Allan told me I should ask you about high school at some point."

"God damn it, Allan." I pulled my hand away from Asher so I could run both over my hair, feeling trapped.

"Don't be mad at him," Asher said, looking a little worried. "You know I would have ended up asking you about it at some point anyway."

"Yyyy... yeah," I said distractedly, feeling a little as if I were back in the police station and about to give evidence for the fourth time. I dropped one hand to my thigh so I could keep tapping a finger there, which I hadn't done in a while, but helped a little when I knew I was going to be stuttering a bunch. "Mm. Okay. Eighth grade. Sssss. Suh. Sahhh. *Soccer*." Damn.

"You get a tuhhh... two-for-one." Asher looked puzzled, and I went on, "There were t-t-*two* guys I got hung up on to sss-start. Just s-started thinking a lot about how they played, what they looked llll... l-l-like. How good it felt when wuhhh... we won, got to celebrate t-together."

I looked down at the table, tapping, tapping on my thigh. Thinking about the smell of wet, torn grass. The look of a smear of mud across the back of a calf. Laughter, a sweaty hug after a game. Arms slung across shoulders, heads pressed together.

I didn't feel comfortable saying any of that, and looked up at Asher hesitantly after the silence had hung in place for a while. The afternoon sun was full in his face, and his expression was dreamy, warm, as if he could see what I was thinking about. He was leaning back in his wheelchair, absent-mindedly running his hand up and down the forearm of his small arm, occasionally pushing up to stretch the bent wrist joint. After another moment, he said slowly, "What did they look like?"

"Oh, god. Um. One was p-p-pretty short. Brown hair. Kind of neat and quick—really quick and fun to watch on offense. He had freckles. Made me lll... laugh a lot. He always had ssss... suh... something surprising to say. Like... I still try to r-r-remember some of his jokes, and I just... I c-can't."

"Ssss... some of that might just be me t-trying to forget things." I said it as lightly as I could, but Asher twisted his mouth to one side. "But it's also... he just thought about things so d-d-differently."

Again, I paused, thinking.

"Other was tall—lot taller than me then. I didn't g-g-grow till later." That made Asher push himself up in his chair straighter, almost grinning. He was excited to have found out something extra about me when I was younger, I realized, embarrassed. I pushed onward. "Um, blond hair. Tan. Kind of cuhhhh—careless. Very cool, I guess. Had kind of long hair, would always—" I tossed my head back at an angle to get imaginary hair out of my eyes. Again, Asher grinned appreciatively.

I had never told anyone else this much. I was ashamed to realize that my heart was actually beating faster out of nervousness. But all the same, it felt nice, safe, knowing that I could just tell Asher, knowing that he'd listen, he'd get it. But I kept to myself the fact that Cyrus, who we'd seen at the library, the day I ended up telling Asher about how I used to sleep around a lot... I'd liked Cyrus a lot more than I should have, considering how he ended up treating me. And a lot of the problem was, from the first time I'd seen him, I couldn't help thinking how much he looked like the blond boy on the soccer team. The measuring way they both had of looking at things—a long, scanning look followed by a private smile, a quick glance away, as if they'd figured out something secret. I didn't and did want him to figure me out, that boy from eighth grade.

"Man." I leaned back a bit and rubbed a hand around the back of my neck, shaking my head slightly. I didn't know how long I'd drifted off.

"So what happened?" Asher asked, softly.

Being gay got shitty, I wanted to say, but didn't. I pressed my tapping finger into my thigh with extra force. "I duhhh..." My voice evaporated out into a useless exhalation, and I had to pause, swallow, breathe, and start again. "I... I d-d-d-didn't really know what was going on. I wasn't thinking about it that much. So someone f-figured it out b-b-before me. Because I watched so much...

"People started b-being shitty to me. M-m-m-my stutter got really shhh... shitty. It was only a l-little problem, off and on, before that." I couldn't help the bitterness that took over my voice. "But it got *really* bad, s-so that was another excuse to fff... fuck with me. After a year or s-something—felt like for-ever—I gave up and quit soccer. Still terrible, next few years. Didn't get better until I started punching people, around the same tuhh... t-t-time I started growing. Last few years of high school—didn't talk to anyone, just worked, got the hell out, kept working.

"Only good thing that whole t-t-time was I think my p-parents heard things, but they... didn't really suhhh... say any-thing, one way or the other. They always had a lll... lot of other stuff t-t-to deal with." I shrugged awkwardly, looked up again.

The way Asher was looking at me then—it was so much better than if he'd said anything. The tenderness.

After another few moments, though, I had to look away again. I propped both elbows on the table, linked my hands to-gether, pressed my mouth against them. I took a deep breath, and another one. I wanted to think about nothing for a little while. My head felt hot.

I heard him say softly from across the table, "I'm so sorry. I can imagine, but... I'll never have *really* gone through some-thing like that."

I shrugged, looking out the window. "Fffff... f-f-feels... like it h-happened to s-s-someone else."

Younger Roy. Dumber Roy. A blank-faced kid who thought he could just blend into the background, couldn't imagine why anyone would want to hurt him, thought that if he just went empty and quiet it would eventually go away. Laundry being put through a spin cycle—that was how I thought of it after a while. Just go blank and let the machine rattle and roar around you, until finally it came to a rest again.

Roy back then had no idea of the importance of strength, of being dense inside yourself. A dense, resilient material that resisted just by existing. That hurt the striker when struck.

I was looking at Asher now, watching his eyes, watching him wait for me: gentle, curious, yet not overexpectant. My finger was tapping against my thigh. I wanted to tell him these things, too, but it was too hard, physically. I had opened my mouth to say something, a while ago, and finally now I closed it, shaking my head.

If not now, later. I could always tell him later. I knew that; his eyes told me that.

But for a second, then, it occurred to me to wonder if Asher would have liked me better if I hadn't had to go through the laundry machine, if I hadn't come out harder, defiant.

I discarded that thought with impatience—impatience, and something like pride. Staring down that stretch of the past, I couldn't stay interested in hypotheticals. What mattered was that I had gotten out. I wasn't proud of everything in my past, I had already told him that once. But I was proud enough of where I had arrived.

As if hearing that thought, Asher leaned across the table to touch my hand. The lightness and coolness of his touch was startling, somehow. "Wanna get out of here?" He made it sound mischievous, though his eyes were concerned.

I pushed back against the table, shaking my head to clear it. I managed a smile. "Yes please."

We left a huge tip for Teddy. As he wiped down the table, he grinned shyly and said we should come see his DJ set later that week at some place I'd never heard of. I tried to sound encouraging, but not overly committed. He got us the ramp again, and we headed out into the afternoon, back into the wind, back down the slope of Charleton.

We took it slow; this part of the hill was so steep that I knew it would make Asher nervous, even with his seatbelt, and even with him taking to the street to avoid the cobblestoned sidewalks.

I felt like I'd been wrenched back into the past and out again. Every time I glanced down at Asher by my side, I felt as if I were seeing him clearly for the first time. The light flickering in his hair as the wind tore at his curls. The fine shape of his upper lip. The way the afternoon sun made his skin look more golden. Once, just to touch him, I reached out to uselessly push some hair back over his ear. He started, his knees drawing up, but then quickly turned his head to touch his lips to the back of my hand. We smiled at each other. When I put my hand back in my jacket pocket, it was almost trembling with the desire to keep touching him.

A few blocks away from the bottom of the hill, we stopped, silent. We turned, and stared down the blind alleyway where Asher had been attacked, and I had found him.

In the daylight together, coming out on the other side of the arraignment, the alleyway looked smaller to me than it had that night, when it had held so much. Somehow now it looked flat, shallow, like a theater set. Anonymous brick buildings on either side.

Set low into the back wall, where I had held up William Riley, there was a half-height metal door, painted black, that must have led into a cellar. I hadn't noticed it that night. I had a sudden surreal impulse to stride down and knock on the door, see where it led. Would it open back up on that night?

I shook my head slightly and looked down. Asher was holding his hand to his throat, pinching the fabric of his scarf between thumb and forefinger, twisting it slowly. The line of his mouth was drawn flat. I watched his face, the fingers of his small hand flexing in and out.

Finally he, too, shook his head, and then sighed. He reached for my hand, and said, "Don't we have a bus to catch?"

16

Be Where You Are

Back at his apartment, I barely let Asher get into the kitchen before I needed to touch him. As the front door swung shut behind me, I leaned forward to wrap my arms around him from behind, reaching down to run my hands down his chest. Just as I kissed the side of his neck, I heard him gasp, felt him tense. His contracted arm clenched up against me.

Quickly I released him, stepping forward to crouch down at one side of his chair and look up into his face. "Sorry," I said hastily. The startled expression was still fading from his face. He shook his head, laughed a little awkwardly. His CP—and, I suspected, his experience in the alleyway—made him jumpy, physically easy to startle. He often tried to apologize for it, so I was pleased when, this time, he didn't. Though I wondered also if he was thinking back to the morning of the arraignment, when he had turned suddenly cold and strange after I'd tried to touch his hand.

If I was thinking of it, he probably was, too.

I reached up to put one hand on his cheek, stretched out my thumb to slowly rub the corner of his mouth. I had a half-formed thought: touch could be strange, unreliable, but it could it also be its own solution. Asher closed his eyes, and then reached to wrap his hand around the back of my neck, pulled me up for a kiss.

His lips were cool. I kissed them, slowly, until they warmed. My heart beat hard, thudding in my chest, anticipating. I could feel him smile against my lips, and then he kissed his way down to my jawline, pausing once to just brush his lips over my stubble. Then he bit my jaw, delicately.

I had to take a long breath, almost shuddering.

I opened my eyes a moment before he did. He flicked his eyes up at me through his lashes. *What*, his look said, *are you going to do now?*

I shifted until I was kneeling in front of him. His smile still looked nervous, but his eyes were glinting. I reached out and slowly slid my hands under his scarf, for a moment felt the warm skin, the tremor that ran through him at my touch, then pulled out to loosen the scarf. Without moving my eyes from his, I dropped the scarf to one side. I undid his jacket, pushed it back over his shoulders, helped him slide it off his good arm first, then eased the other, bunched sleeve off of his bent arm. Everywhere I moved, I paused to touch, stroke, as if I were molding him for the first time. His body moved restlessly.

His jacket, too, we dropped to the floor; and then his shirt, and mine. For a moment I sat back on my heels, just looking at him. Asher. Dark-haired, bare-chested, flushed, breathing deeply, his lips parted. Looking half embarrassed, half thrilled, exposed there in his kitchen. The slanting afternoon light cast a wash of shadow below his cheekbones, his jaw, his upraised arm, even the hollows of his ribs. Every time his legs kicked, thrusting, or a spasm ran through his abdomen, the shadows flickered, smoothly sliding off over the planes of his body.

My eyes couldn't stop moving over him, his vividness. Suddenly my mind flicked back to the arraignment —when the men had come into the courtroom, the way I had seen it all in heated, jagged flashes. How strangely similar this moment felt, and how different. The way I wanted to stay here, watch this moment of him breathing, moving, waiting, over and over again.

The restfulness of it. The hunger.

Slowly, I moved my hands to his waist. I stroked my fingers there, one at a time. I leaned to kiss him, as he reached his arm to stroke my neck, my back, slid down to grip my ass with sudden strength. I hummed appreciatively, slid my lips down his neck, just barely touching, until I rested them where I could feel the play of his muscles as his right shoulder twitched, subtly.

Feeling that, it suddenly, finally, occurred to me to ask: "How's your back?"

Asher burst out laughing, pushed my shoulder back so that he could see my face. "*Now* you ask?" he demanded. I shrugged, flushing, ducking my face back down.

"Sweet Roy," he said. I heard him unbuckling his seatbelt, and then there was a sudden warm weight on my head: he had leaned forward to drape himself over me. "Look at your face. Sorry, I shouldn't have laughed." He kissed my ear. "It's okay. I took a *lot* of muscle relaxants the rest of the week."

He said all of this in a murmur. The part of my brain that wasn't consumed with embarrassment thought about how much I liked it that Asher always spoke so softly when we were together like this. I'd been with men who just kept *talking* in normal, even bored, voices in the bedroom.

Asher kissed my ear again, rubbed his fingertips along the nape of my neck. "And how," he said, "are you?"

I felt warm, and the words came out easily, almost thoughtlessly. "Good. Great. It's so easy to focus when I'm with you." I had told him that the worst part of using sex had been how mechanical it had become. Going through the motions, chasing down the expected chemical hit. Half the time already distracted and dissatisfied within the first five minutes of starting anything.

I felt Asher's warm exhale. "You don't know how happy that makes me to hear."

Still bent under his comfortable weight, I pressed my hands into his waist again, then slid my fingers under the waistband of his jeans and into the hollows under his hipbones. He gasped, and I couldn't help smiling to myself at the expected kick of his legs.

I curled my fingertips into the sensitive skin at the bend of his hips, moved to stroke the now-familiar stretch of surgical scar tissue. Asher sighed.

After another moment, I whispered, "Sit up again?" He complied, pushing himself back off of me and leaning back in his chair with a heavy-lidded smile.

I slid my hands back out against his hips, and then, in unspoken accord, we each moved to undo each other's jeans. But we were daring each other to move as deliberately, as minutely as we could, pausing often to stroke, to smile, to give looks that said, *I could take all day, doing this*. I felt so buoyed up with anticipation that it was if I was outside of myself.

Finally Asher gave up the game—or maybe won it. Grinning, he swiftly tugged down my jeans and boxers. Still kneeling, I was moving awkwardly to extract my legs, when he leaned forward again and took me deeply into his mouth.

I had been thinking so much about him all day that I nearly came, just then. But he must have known, because he *hmm*ed deep in his throat, moved his tongue against me just once, with careful slowness, and then withdrew, grinning again.

I groaned; I closed my eyes. Still thinking about the feeling of his mouth on me, resenting the now suddenly cold air, I slowly sat, pulled my pants off the rest of the way, kicked aside my shoes and socks. I took in a deep, shuddering breath and opened my eyes again.

With playful vengeance, I stripped Asher in turn, briefly and so easily lifting him from his chair to complete the process of taking off his jeans that he laughed. I set him back down again, tossed the jeans onto the growing tangle on the kitchen floor, and kissed him roughly, his lips, his shoulders. I ran my hands down one of his thin legs, now stopping to kiss his knee, the slight swell of his calf. I circled my hands around his ankle, slid down to the inwards-bent foot. Here I slowed. Whenever I really thought about it, there was still something surreal about realizing that he had never been able to stand—it was simply so different from anything I had ever experienced. But at the same time, it was a fact I had already absorbed, that this was the Asher I knew, and he had never known or been any differently, either.

I ran my hands over his stiff ankle joint, his curled foot, whose sole had never been able to touch the ground. It jerked and tugged gently in my grasp as his legs stirred.

From the tense quality of his silence, I could tell Asher was getting uncomfortable with this attention, but I left my fingers there for another moment before placing a kiss on the top of his foot and gently releasing it. "I just like seeing you," I said in explanation when I looked up again.

"Oh, well," he said, a little breathlessly, his previously un-comfortable smile warming.

"Work by this c-criminally underappreciated artist..." I murmured, quoting—it was a joke, sort of, that Asher liked to make about himself sometimes. Asher was the "work." The "artist" was the god of people with disabilities.

Asher grinned shyly and reached to run his hand along the outside edge of my hip, and then back down to cup my ass.

"Mmm. C-can I pick you up?"

"Yes, please," he said.

"Let's try..." I picked him up with one arm under his thighs and one hand behind his back, tried to wrap his legs around me so that I could hold him chest-to-chest with me—but stopped when his thighs suddenly clenched tight around me, and he winced. "Mm, maybe another time," I said quickly, at the same time that Asher apologized. For a moment we looked down wistfully at the gap between us: his hips were still far too tight for us to be able to embrace this way.

"So close yet so far..." Asher murmured, still looking down.

"Mm-hm. D-d-don't worry. Plenty other things we can try." I turned and started walking slowly to the bedroom, enjoying the way he was playing his fingers over the back of my neck again.

"Like this?"

I gasped, and then sighed: Asher had dropped his hand down to start rubbing me slowly.

"Oh, yes."

Without stopping, Asher leaned forward and rested his forehead against my shoulder. "Keep walking—keep going. And I'll keep going."

***

We lay in bed. It was weirdly nice, luxurious, to be naked in bed together with a little daylight still in the sky, the blue of twilight only just approaching. It was as if we'd won extra weekend.

We'd played, napped, and then played again. Both of us had been determined to make it last, keeping it slow, pausing often just to kiss and touch each together, letting the suspense stretch on and on.

The second round, especially, had spun out into a kind of lazy experimentation, continuing the process of figuring out what Asher could and couldn't do, exploring his physical limits. Without talking about it, both of us knew that this was the best time for us to really experiment. After the initial urgency was out of the way, Asher felt less pressure, so he was less tense, less self-conscious.

I was also starting to realize that the process put me into a weirdly enjoyable problem-solving mindset, and I thought Asher had noticed, too, from the teasingly serious way that he'd ask me for suggestions.

As we lazed together afterward, he had started threatening to go back to his physical therapist with a suspiciously specific list of requests. "It's either that, or you'll have to become my personal trainer."

"Is this *not* personal training already? Maybe..." I nipped his ear, and he laughed in protest, "...you sh-sh-should be paying me."

"Hmm, I certainly wouldn't call it *im*personal... Do you think," he said consideringly, "they would give you a discount at the boxing store if you only had to buy one glove? For when you *really* start whipping me into shape." Slowly, he punched a displaced pillow that lay in front of him.

"There's no such thing as a boxing store."

"Oh, yeah? Then where do all the boxes come from?"

I sighed loudly.

"This is a real turning point in our relationship, Roy. I'd been restraining myself from making that joke for *so long*. Now it's gone. We can never go back to the way things were."

I sighed again, and slid my hand up from the side of his face to loosely cover his mouth in a mock reprimand, as he shook with laughter. He twisted his head a little, so that one of my fingertips slid into his mouth. He licked it.

"Hm. Careful," I warned him, "do you really have the sss... s-stamina for World War III?"

"Is that what we're calling it now?"

"That's it. I'm out of funny," I said, nestling more deeply into the mattress, and pulling him more tightly to me. "You have sss... sole r-responsibility for dumb jokes for the rest of the evening."

"What a heavy burden to bear..." His voice trailed off sleepily.

Again we drifted off. Dusk filled the room with blue light.

A little while later, we stirred at the same time, slightly disentangling ourselves. The sun had set, and it felt pleasantly den-like in Asher's dark bedroom. I had the vague sense that he had been awake for longer than me. I must have felt his legs starting to move again, before I'd been all the way awake.

I kissed the back of his neck, then made space for him as he started to push himself onto his back. He smiled at me without saying anything, watching me stretch. Then his gaze grew absent.

After a little while, I said, "Asher..."

"Hm?"

"D-d-duhh... d-do you want to tell me... what you were th-thinking about the arraignment?"

"How did you know that's what I was thinking about?" he said with artificial brightness. I didn't bother responding.

He held the not-smile for another moment, then turned his head so he was looking up at the ceiling and sighed heavily. "Sorry for being so vague about everything. I know you've been worrying."

I made a noncommittal noise. I reached to hold his left hand, loosely, and he gave a brief squeeze of acknowledgement.

He paused, his eyes tracking back and forth across the ceiling.

"Okay. One thought: Everything Ms. Ganon said to me on the phone, about not standing up for myself, or for the disabled community... I already thought that myself, at least ten times." His voice was slow, every word placed uncomfortably.

"Another thought: Also, I just... really, really want everything not to have happened. Except for the part where I met you."

There was a long pause. Asher's legs moved jerkily under the covers.

He continued: "It's just... it's a really fucked up thing to have happened. You know how I don't even like other people to touch my joystick, or push me without asking, let alone..." He trailed off, and I watched as he swallowed, his throat making a dry click.

When he spoke again, his voice was so vehement that I almost flinched. "You do all this work, telling yourself that you're strong, you're independent. That your disability is more a problem with society than with you. Okay, so then what? You're still society's victim, whenever it... it forgets its manners." His voice was heavy with scorn, anger, in a way I had never heard before. "Whenever some guy from the Internet realizes he's disgusted by your body. Or some assholes decide a wheelchair is a fucking toy, not somebody's legs. Or—or—" I shifted as he gripped my hand with sudden intensity and jerked his head to the side on the pillow to look at me. "Or some asshole *kids* decide it's fun to torture another kid because he *might* be gay, oh *and* he has a stammer. Ha fucking ha."

My stomach curled in on itself in a way that felt like fear— an old fear. I had to push it aside.

"Just—fuck!" Asher let go of my hand to gesture wildly, and then dropped his hand down onto his forehead. In the dim light from the window, I could see his eyes darting back and forth, no longer meeting mine. "*Why* why why does my health, or your sanity, or—or anybody's, have to depend on what the shittiest people in the world decide they're going to do for fun that Tuesday."

He gave a long, shaky exhale, and reached down to find my hand again. "Sorry."

I murmured a reassurance, waiting, holding myself still.

He continued, somewhat more slowly, "Like, good job, district attorney's office. Good job, criminal justice system. Good job cleaning up after this mess, I guess. But is it so crazy to just want none of it to have happened in the first place? Just think about how much *time* we would have saved." The sarcasm in his voice was so intense that it bordered on another emotion, one I couldn't name.

"Ms. Ganon thinks I should sue for emotional damages. What would be really great would be if I could sue to not *have* any emotional damages. But something tells me that's not how things work."

He fell silent. He stared off at the window. His eyes were steady again, and the jerking of his legs was slowing.

Finally he looked back at me. "I don't know if that went anywhere. Sorry."

I had still been digesting, considering. But now I felt a hot surge of protective affection. I rolled and wrapped my arm around his narrow chest, holding tightly, feeling his warmth, the sudden flexion as a spasm ran through him. My other hand still held on to his; I stroked my thumb over the back of his hand. "Asher, why do you apologize for everything?"

I looked up in time to see his face go blank. Then he gave an uncomfortable "Umm..."

"I'm not chhh... changing the subject," I added hastily. "I just..." I thought for a moment. "I want you to be able to be pissed off if you want. Or hurt. Or even... just not apologizing b-b-because you think you're in people's way, but you're not actually. Or maybe you are, but you can't help it, so, so what. Screw them." I aimed to say it playfully, and was pleased, or relieved, when Asher laughed. "But seriously. You said it: there are a lot of assholes. You deserve to take up s-s-sss... *space*. Sidewalks. Wherever." I kissed his cheek. He looked more pleased than I thought I deserved.

I paused, thinking again. What I wanted to say next, I was less comfortable with. "I know I'm not always... open, my-self. So I hope this doesn't sound... fuhhh... f-f-f-fake. But it mm-matters to me when you tell me things like this. And it matters to me when I sss... see that you're h-hurting, or afraid. I don't always know what to say. Usually I just want to hold you." Resting my forehead against his cheek, I could feel him smiling.

"So..." Again I had to pause, feeling as if I had already used up all my good ideas. "Just... honestly, it feels reassuring just to hear you s-s-s-say, 'that was fucked up.' I feel like that must be th-th-the most you've talked about it since the night I actually f-found you."

"It's gotten kind of... wound up, in here," he admitted.

"Mm. And it *doesn't* feel reassuring when the only other thing I s-see is... you having nnn... nightmares." I said it as gently as I could, looking at his face again, knowing the likeli-hood he'd take it as another kind of guilt to hold. He grimaced and pushed his face into my shoulder. I could feel that his cheeks were hot.

I continued in the same tone, "Look, I know your m-m-mom has already been on you about it. B-b-but I haven't really said anything yet. So: if you feel like you want more help figur-ing thhh... things out—can you please look for help? I want to h-help, but I'm not even a g-g-good everyday talker. Let alone a professional talker." I nudged him with the shoulder he was leaning into. "That's what they call it, right? P-professional talker?"

He laughed so shakily that I realized with a jolt of alarm that he was actually crying a little. But his body was quiet. "Sorry. No, I mean I'm *not* sorry." I smiled, despite my concern. "Yes. Yes." Awkwardly he reached his left arm up from under my overlapping arm to rub his face, sniffing. "I, Asher, promise you, Roy, to either share more things with you than nightmares... or find a professional talker."

"Or both..." I suggested tentatively. Everything I'd managed to say had been reasonable enough, I thought, but I was way out of my comfort zone here. I was reaching for scattered memories of the one guy I'd been with who talked with what seemed to me to be alarming casualness about "getting help for things."

"Or both," Asher agreed. "Mmmf." He was sitting up, carefully pushing himself up in a way that suggested his back was bothering him again. "Can you hold me?"

I blinked at him, distracted by the need to search his face for remaining tears. But he just looked a little flushed, blotchy. "How?"

"In your lap," he said shyly.

"Oh!" I smiled and pushed myself up too, looked to make sure he was ready, then reached to draw him into my lap. At the same time I pulled my legs up so they were bent at the same angle as his, supporting him. With the warmth of his full body against me, I sighed contentedly, put my arms around his chest.

"Oh my god," he said at the same time. "You're like the best heating pad in the world."

"That's me. Did we hurt your b-b-back?"

"Just a little twinge-y."

"Well I don't know how *that* could have hhhh... happened," I said, kissing the side of his neck, enjoying the way the dim light from the windows caught his collarbones.

"It's a great mystery," he agreed, very low in his throat, and reached up to lace his fingers into mine. Once again I felt a jolt of desire; he laughed appreciatively.

"Unstable ground," I warned him.

"Hmmm," he said speculatively. Slowly, he arched his back against me a little; it could have been an innocent stretch.

"Mmm. Does *this* count as th-therapy?"

"Oh, I thought we'd established that already. Really, your therapeutic commitment is... commendable."

I snorted. Again I kissed him from the side. Then I tipped his chin until I could see his eyes. "You *really* want to...?"

He laughed, embarrassed. "Yeah, you got me. Honestly, I'm starving."

I laughed, too. "Me too." It had been a long afternoon, and a long time since those fries at Zeke's. "'Kay. Refuel. Then we go back to... wh-whatever."

"Whatever," Asher agreed happily. "Take me to the bathroom? And then bring me my chair?"

"Mm-hm..." I was already shifting him so I could climb out of bed with him in my arms, my mind racing ahead. His warm weight felt light, so light; the best weight to carry. The weekend was drawing to an end, but there were still so many hours left in the night.

17 |

Orion

Over the weeks that followed, Asher swore more, got into moods, twice even started crying unexpectedly. We had our first arguments during this time, over little things, practical things, places where we just didn't see eye-to-eye in conversations—usually Asher pushing me on stuff that I just couldn't see was a problem, no matter how I tried to wrap my head around it.

I knew he needed stuff left just right in his apartment—chargers and appliances where he could reach them, nothing in the way of his typical wheelchair routes—so I was always careful to copy the patterns he'd set, and always ready to go on fishing expeditions to retrieve anything that had rolled away under furniture. I wanted him to be able to use his space without thinking twice about any of it. But in those weeks, Asher constantly seemed to be shifting the goalposts. He'd insist that I'd moved his toothbrush (I had, because he'd asked me to take it back to the bathroom for him), plugged a charger in the wrong outlet (I hadn't), or that this had been the right corner to leave my shoes *last* week, but now, for reasons he didn't want to have to explain, this corner no longer made any sense.

I had never been picky about my own stuff or space, but I understood why Asher needed to be. I didn't *want* any of this to be a big deal, but it was exhausting to constantly be renegotiating so many details. And it almost seemed to make him more annoyed that when he'd correct me, all I'd do was say, "Okay, sorry," and make a mental note to get it right—the *new* right—next time.

I didn't know what kind of reaction he was looking for, but he'd keep pushing and pushing on the same detail, and I'd stand there, not knowing what else to say, feeling more and more oversized, useless, and in the way.

A dispute over the doormat went like this:

Asher told me that if I opened the front door and it dragged the doormat out of place, I had to slide the doormat back against the threshold.

I said, "Sure, sorry, I can do that." And I slid the door-mat back.

"If you don't, the mat just ends up getting pushed and pulled further away from the door. It, like, migrates."

I nodded.

"And then I have trouble moving it back."

"That makes sense."

"You *know* I have trouble moving it back."

He was staring at me with intent eyes, his brow slightly furrowed, and I just didn't know what the urgency in his look meant. So I nodded again.

"I wish I didn't have to tell you all this stuff."

I reacted with a shrug and a smile, as if his tone had been apologetic, even though it wasn't.

"So you'll remember next time? Sometimes you just kind of... blow into the place."

And so on, until the veiled accusations went on for long enough that finally, I had to tell him, "I don't know what else you want me to say. I'm listening. I'm r-r-really listening. And you c-c-c-can tell me if I get it wrong again. But I d-don't know what else you w-w-want me to *say*."

That was one of the times he started crying.

One second he was staring at me blankly; the next there were tears spilling out of both eyes and down his cheeks, and his mouth was beginning to twist into a grimace. His legs thrust out of his chair. He lifted his hand to one cheek and stared at the moisture left on the tips of his fingers, as if he didn't know where it was coming from. More than anything else, he looked embarrassed, his cheeks flushing and eyebrows drawing together in consternation, but the tears kept coming.

We must have said "I'm sorry" at the same time. I moved to hug him. I kissed the top of his head, and felt his shoulders shake and his small arm jerk against his chest. He said "I'm sorry" again, into my shoulder, and put his arm around me, too. His fingers dug into the back of my shirt.

I didn't know what to do except keep holding him. My stomach turned over and over with guilt and unease.

Maybe you're not cut out, suggested a voice in my head, *for relationships that last longer than a month*. The lazy drawl sounded like Cyrus'. I drew a shutter down on it, pushed it away, until I was only holding Asher, my head empty. I listened to him draw in shaky breaths and blow them away again.

"That actually feels pretty good," he said after a time.

"What?" I pulled back to look at his face.

"Crying," he replied, and gave half a smile. "I tried to stop, but it just... keeps on going. I feel like a faucet that someone left on. But not necessarily in a bad way." He sniffed and smeared tears away with the back of his hand.

I touched his cheek.

"I just..." He drew in another shaky breath. "Ahhh... shit, I don't know. I'm sorry. I don't know why any of this—" and he gestured to the doormat, "—seems to matter so much. I really don't. But... I can't get it out of my head that you're... that you're mad at me. And I guess... it's like I want you to say it."

"Mad at *you*? Asher, I..." My jaw locked up, and I exhaled hard, dropping my hands to my sides. I had to look away, listening to my own breathing now, reaching for the words again and again, my head bobbing as I tried to get them out. I tapped a finger against my thigh impatiently.

I blinked, and finally the block was over. I looked back at Asher. He'd taken the moment to back up his wheelchair a little so that he could reach for a handful of tissues from the kitchen counter. He was wiping his eyes and cheeks now. His tears had slowed, but he still looked raw and unhappy.

"I get... f-f-f-frustrated," I said carefully, "but because I'm confused, not because I'm m-m-mad. At you. I j-j-j-juhhh... juhhhh... I want to know the rr... rr... right thing to do."

Asher set down the crumpled tissues in his lap and bit his lower lip. "Thank you. Thanks, Roy." He paused, then went on with an effort. "I'm sorry, I already know this is going to sound stupid, but... so when you say, 'Okay, sorry'... are you *really* just saying 'okay'?"

I nodded.

"Okay. Okay." He ran his hand through his hair; the ends around his face had gotten damp with tears. He gave an awkward smile. "You just... I just get worried that you look mad, sometimes. Your 'just serious' face is kind of close to your mad face. So I don't always know what your face is doing."

"I don't either," I offered with a shrug, and he laughed a little.

"Okay," he said again, and he reached out his hand to me. I took it and kissed his palm, and he smiled. Then he squared his shoulders, pulling himself up a little in his wheelchair. "I'll try to cool it with the... whatever is making me so goddamn crazy about the, uh, domestic nitpicking. And I'll believe you when you say that it's okay."

"And I'll try not to be so..." I gestured vaguely at my face, flattening my lips out in a grimace.

"No, no," he said, laughing again, and leaning forward to reach for a hug. "I love your face. I need your face to be your face."

I ran my fingers down the tight muscles of his neck, down along the ridge of his spine, and then shifted, pulling away from his hug a little, so that I could hunker down in front of him. I was tired of looming over him, feeling like an oversized clod. I slid my hands down until I could rest them on his knees. He looked into my eyes, and I asked him, "How come you cried?"

He bit his lip again. "I don't know. I felt like I was yelling at you, I guess. And I'm just... stressed. Everything feels off lately. But not you, I mean... It's just weird." He shook his head and shifted in his seat, frowning, looking down at his thighs and pushing against them, stretching his hips. "It's just weird," he repeated, shrugging a little. "But it's not because of something you did."

I watched his brown eyes, his dark lashes still stuck together in spikes with moisture, the residual tremble that occasionally ran through his mouth. I was grateful for the reassurance, but I still knew enough to guess that if Asher was upset with me on some level, it was because of what I *wasn't* doing.

After meeting up a few more times with Amy over the past month, it had been impossible not to notice the way that she offered Asher a constant stream of commentary, opinion, and affirmation, and the way that he seemed to relax into it. When Asher kept pushing me for a response, anything more than a basic acknowledgement, I think what he wanted was *responsiveness.*

I licked my lips and pushed myself. "Well. If... if you n-need more from me, tell me. I can't always s-sss-say a l-l-lot. But I do say w-w-w-what I can think of to say."

From the way he glanced away briefly, I knew I had gotten close to the truth, but neither of us said anything else. He just pulled me close again and kissed each of my cheeks, then my mouth, then excused himself to go wash his face.

***

That conversation cleared the air, made more space for both of us, but it didn't fix everything, of course. Asher was still unpredictable and short-tempered, even if I could see him trying to catch himself once he realized he was getting wound up.

I tried to find more ways to show that I was there, that I was listening. I touched him more often; I'd find breaks during the day to text him a photo of a plant or a "Thinking of you."

I tried to hide it, but I *was* alarmed, worried that something had gone wrong, that I had gotten something wrong on a fundamental level. The phrase *he's too good for you* started floating into my head with disturbing frequency. I strained to avoid going as far as, *He* thinks *he's too good for you.* Had his parents—no matter how sweet they were to my face—said something about me?

But after another couple of weeks, I realized—I think we both realized—how much of Asher's calm and cheerfulness over the past couple of months had actually been forced. He'd been spinning his wheels furiously trying to maintain his composure, focusing on his job, his parents, Amy, and, I realized now—the work of our relationship, the work of starting something between two people who, at the end of the day, came from really different places. Looking back, I thought I could see places where I now recognized the intensity of his focus, even his way of caring for me, as a little frantic, strained.

Watching the arraignment had opened the way for something to sweep through him. Stress, anger, fear. It set both of us back on our heels.

Something else I remembered from early on in our relationship: I'd gotten angry about something stupid, a client who kept wanting to renegotiate the contract when we were already halfway done with the work, something like that. Even as worked up as I was then, I had to notice the spasms that had started to overtake Asher's body. My anger was making him uncomfortable.

He noticed me noticing, and he made an awkward joke: he was taking notes from me, because sometimes he didn't even know how to be angry.

I was realizing now that it hadn't been a joke. Slowly, very slowly, I was realizing that some of the things about him that I'd thought of as deeply characteristic—mainly his ability to take hard things and force a conversation about them—were actually taxing for him, even exhausting. And those conversations seemed to eat at him afterwards, in a way they didn't for me. Maybe it was a habit I'd had to learn in high school, but

I mostly felt like once something had happened, I could take a breath and then just step away.

There was one particularly tense evening when we were out at a restaurant together and it was clear that Asher was exhausted by a day of bad spasms and really just wanted to go home. I asked him two or three times, but even then he refused to admit it, just sat there looking tense and closed-off. Alone in my apartment afterward, frustrated, thinking things over, I wondered if some of the way that Asher tended to present himself as open, someone who easily spread his emotions around, was really a reflection of how *Amy* liked to present herself. She was obviously the more outgoing of the two, found it easy to let it out and let it go. In his own ways, Asher was almost as private, secretive as I was.

But we adjusted. Things between us shifted, resettled, shifted again. After enough trial and error, I found myself thinking that it almost felt like we had started our relationship over again. That something that had shown itself in glimpses between us before, was now beginning to flow steadily. I hadn't even realized I could want anything else from Asher. But I liked these glints of newness.

I got more used to pushing him to talk, when it was clear he couldn't get over that barrier himself—the way he had, I knew, done it for me before. No matter how stiff and unnatural I felt, his gratitude afterwards was so obvious that it pushed both of us to keep going with it.

And he did find a therapist. He didn't talk about that much, either, but sometimes I thought I could see him trying out new things, new ways of thinking about things.

One night, maybe two weeks after he'd first told me that he'd started seeing a therapist, Asher asked if he could tell me something. We were lazing on his living room couch after long work days for both of us. He sat across my lap, leaning against the armrest. Outside, a persistent wind gusted around the corners of the building, driving a fine rain against the windows.

"You know," Asher said, "the scars on my hips?"

"Mm-hm..."

He drove straight to the point. After he'd had that surgery, Asher said, he'd been in so much pain that he'd ended up severely depressed. It was supposed to be a straightforward operation, one that would correct growing issues with his posture and make transfers easier for him, but afterward it was so bad that he could barely sleep, couldn't stand to use his chair for more than a few hours a day. He ended up moving back in with his parents, missing a semester of college, then a year—something he'd mentioned a few times before, just not the reason.

"It was so bad. It was *so* bad, Roy," he said, staring down as he slowly stretched out his right thumb and wrist. "And it just felt so pointless. And preventable. You know?"

"Yes. But you c-c-couldn't have known, when you said yes. But even after all of that... d-d-d... d-did it help?"

"*Nope.*"

I swore.

He went on, "The definition of pointless. It was a lot... it took a lot of work to get over feeling betrayed. Even after things got back on track, I got into this loop where I was determined never to feel that bad again, at the same time that I was convinced something was going to happen. Sooner or later... You see where I'm going with this."

"Yes. Yes. I'm sorry, Asher." I pressed my lips against the side of his head, not exactly thinking, more seeing how everything fit together. He didn't say anything else for a bit, just pressed up against the palm of his contracted hand, watching the way it loosened his fingers to move more freely, as if seeing it for the first time.

Finally I said, more lightly, "We've seen some shit."

"Many flavors," he agreed, "if not all." For the first time in a while, he looked up again. "But you know what, I feel pretty good about things lately."

I smiled, leaned my head to one side. "G-good. Me too."

"Even if I haven't always been showing it, lately." He quirked his mouth, but I shrugged and hugged him.

"We'll figure it out," I said, and released him. After another moment I said, "So what do you want to do this winter?" I nudged his back with the arm he was leaning against.

He made a face, glanced back at one of the windows where rain still came pattering in fitful gusts. "Isn't it winter already? It sounds awful out."

"Doesn't c-c-count till it snows." Again, he made a face. "I know, it sss... sucks for you. Sorry." He anticipated my apologetic kiss, and turned his head to catch my lips with his. "Hm.

Well, either way, I thhhhh... I th... I think we should do something you've never done before."

"*Me?* Why does it have to be me?"

"Okay, both of us."

He burst out laughing and finally stopped fidgeting with his hands, dropping his left hand back into his lap. "That was *so* insincere. You just want me to go with you to the gym with you or something."

"No," I said stubbornly, "you've already done that."

"Okay, you want me to go with the gym with you and... get into a fistfight with some MMA guy. Who looks like Brad Pitt in *Fight Club.*"

"*Now* you're talking."

"No! Dammit, Roy..."

"Ready...?" I had shifted him so that I clasped his back to my chest.

"Dammit—yes—" He laughed helplessly, his left hand tightly gripping my wrist, and I twisted so that I more or less fell to the floor in a loose crouch, Asher sheltered inside the curve of my body. I briefly took the shock of the fall with my feet before rolling backwards to rock up and down on my back.

"*Takedown,*" I whispered into his hair. He kept laughing as I gradually rocked to a stop, his legs jerking in and out with his excitement.

"You're the worst," he said finally.

"B-but also..."

"But also the best. ...Yeah. Let's do some things this winter. Get drunk. Climb a mountain. Get *you* in a fight. Go on a road trip. See an opera."

"Don't get *too* crazy now."

"No, let's *do* things."

"We will. We will."

***

"He *is* a softie, isn't he? Here, have some more." Amy was thrusting the pitcher in my direction, sending a little splash of amber-colored liquid over the lip, but her glinting eyes were fixed on the other side of the room, on Roy.

"What is this? What are we drinking?"

"It's supposed to taste like apple pie. Asher, give me your glass."

"Yes, but what's in it?"

"I don't know. Cinnamon. Rum. Apple pie juice."

"Oh god. Fine, here—" I relinquished my glass, and Amy refilled it with a grandiosely generous pour. "What were you saying again?" Our any-holiday party had been going for hours at this point, and her snug, dimly lit apartment was a few degrees below uncomfortably warm. Couples and trios—work friends, a few college friends—were crammed wherever they could find a spot to sit or lean in the furniture-cluttered living room. The dining table was piled with food and the somewhat self-conscious assortment of mismatched holiday décor that we requested that every guest contribute to: a wicker reindeer, an electric menorah (mine), a hand turkey scribbled on copy paper, and the winner of that year's "Most Culturally Confusing" award: a shamrock piñata, triumphantly discovered in a dust-clogged back shelf of a dollar store. A thread of bell-filled jazz occasionally made itself audible above the constant chatter.

I felt sleepy, suffused with a sense of goodwill that was so total that on some level I was worried about how chemically induced it might be. But I had to admit that it made a nice change from the anxiety that had grown so frequent in my chest that fall that its absence was confusing. Automatically I put the glass to my lips again once Amy handed it back to me. It did taste like apple pie.

"Roy," Amy persisted. "He's a softie." She bounced her own almost-empty glass against one of her shins. I followed her gaze: across the room, Roy was more or less trapped behind a couch, leaning against the corner of the back wall with his legs crossed. He rubbed his upper lip with one finger as his gaze moved around the room slowly. A beer bottle dangled from the fingers of his other hand. My chest loosened with emotion as I watched him. Without thinking about it, I sighed.

"Look at him," Amy said, seeming to agree. "He's so worried. Is he having enough fun that he's not offending us? Should he be meeting more people? It's like he's gotten out of the swimming pool and is trying to figure out if he should get back in."

"Be nice," I said automatically, without any real edge. It was just that on top of his usual difficulties, I knew that parties made Roy nervous because his voice was so low that it didn't carry all that well.

Amy put a hand on my arm. "I am. I am. I promise. I genuinely think it's sweet. He's so sincere. Are you guys gonna get married?"

"Oh my gosh, Amy." Normally I would have been mortified, but just now I felt absurdly pleased, though I did my best to sound indignant.

"Look at your *face!*" She exclaimed so loudly that a pair of girls near us turned to look, raising their eyebrows with amusement as I shushed her frantically. "What, did he propose to you already?"

"No, oh my gosh. I protest this injustice, Amy. I don't bug you about Vikram all the time."

In fact, I *did* feel, in the weirdest way, as if I'd been proposed to. That morning, Roy had asked me what I would think if he traded in his pick-up for a van.

"A van?" I said distractedly; I was "managing" my anxiety by triple-checking the grocery list for the party, trying to hold off a disproportionately gloomy sense of impending failure.

"You know," Roy said, "a... a... a wuhh. A wheelchair van."

I put down my phone and stared up at him. He was flushing deeply. He went on hastily, "I j-j-just feel like we w-waste a lot of time at bus stops, and a lot of money on cabs. It would be mmm... mm. *More* efficient to. You know. Ride around together."

I pushed my hand down on my joystick until my chair bumped up against Roy's shins. "Oof," he said quietly. I leaned forward to hug him around his middle.

"It's too much," I said, my face pushed into his flannel shirt. "But yes. I'd love it. If you're sure it would work—you'd be able to fit all your work stuff in it still?" I looked up at him. It was if wind had blown through my mind: it was clear again, bright.

"Yeah," he said eagerly, "It's easy to take the back seats out, to fit more stuff. It won't be as easy to jjj... just th-throw things in, but—" He shrugged.

"Worst case scenario, I guess you could get a flatbed trailer?" I said slowly, thinking over how he tended to do things. "You know, for the next time someone wants you to put in a 50-year-old oak."

"I *wish* someone would ask m-m-me to put in a 50-year-old oak," Roy said, passionately.

I laughed. "That might be the most excited I've heard you get all week. Even more than about the van." I tightened my arm around him, pressed my face into him again. "One day you'll have to climb a tree with me. Like Tarzan and Jane."

Roy gave a speculative *hmmm*.

"Anyway," I said. "Yes. I would... beyond love it. It feels like a lot. But... as long as you're sure."

"I'm sure," was all he said.

For me, though, it still felt like a piece of happiness too uncertain to put my weight on yet. Amy was squinting at me assessingly now, with an eager little kittenish smile on her lips. But finally she said, "Fine, keep your secrets, Mr. Klein."

"There's even better entertainment afoot," I said, seeing an opportunity for distraction. I poked her leg. "Look—" Across the room, Vikram was slowly making his way through the crowd toward Roy, holding two beers. When he'd finally made it to the back wall, he offered one to Roy, who gratefully set aside his empty and accepted it. Finally, Vikram sort of applied himself carefully to the wall next to Roy, and they bent their heads toward each other in conversation. Vikram was almost as tall as Roy, cleanly built, with a solemn, rectangular face, dark brown complexion, straight black brows and curly hair. It was hard not to admire how they looked, standing together with rather similar attitudes of studied relaxation.

Amy was knocking the back of her hand against my upper arm in wordless excitement. A moment later, she said, "It's happening! It's finally happening!" And then: "What are they *talking* about?"

"I don't know, traditionally masculine things?" I was as curious as her, of course, but it was more fun to tease her. I sat back in my chair to watch, taking the moment to again enjoy the warm sense of physical relaxation that had overtaken me. I was fascinated to realize that I could extend my legs with much more voluntary control than usual, and covertly went on stretching them, one at a time, as Amy kept up a running commentary on our menfolk. I was embarrassed, and then pleased, to realize that I associated this unusual ease of movement with how I felt after having sex with Roy. Now I watched him from across the room with the added glow of desire.

Maybe half an hour later, Roy and I had managed to find our ways back to each other, and I took the chance to ask him about his conversation with Vikram. He responded with a surprisingly direct question: "Did Amy ever have a c-c-crush on you?"

"What? Oh my gosh. Sure, but literally back in high school. And she goes through at least one crush, like, a season. Is that what you *talked* about?"

"No," he said, looking off a little, "Vikram is way too p-p... polite for that. But I could tell it was... under some things he asked me."

"Hmmm," I said, alarmed by how guilty I felt. To distract myself, I pressed Roy, "What else did you talk about?"

He shrugged. "Things."

"Oh I *see*," I said, as if I'd been enlightened. He shrugged again, and then flashed a much more mischievous smile than usual at me. It shook me back into my state of warm delight, and I laughed and reached out to lace my fingers through his; he was leaning over me, perched on the arm of a sofa.

"Anyway," Roy said, "I think Vikram huhhh... has much more immediate competition." I knew what he meant. To the delight of both of us, Allan had been able to make the party, despite the expected jokes about killing the party simply by virtue of being depressingly old, and for the last half an hour or so, he'd been drawing an increasing number of the party toward him, forming a storyteller's ring. He was unspooling a yarn now that I could only hear in snatches, as his voice rose and fell with warm theatricality and his listeners' laughter trailed behind. Snuggled directly to his left was Amy, with both her arms loosely wrapped around his upper arm and her head leaning on his shoulder, her belly laugh rising above the others'.

"Isn't he just in his element," I said to Roy. He snorted in agreement, smiling.

There was something magical about it all; I leaned forward, grasping Roy's hand harder, and then planted a kiss on his knuckles.

"Hey," said a loud voice. Both of us looked around, startled. "Hey," it said again. It was one of Amy's work friends, a woman with dark curly hair and deep-set eyes. I thought her name was Alisa, Iliza, something like that. "Are you guys *together*?" Roy and I looked at each other, and then back at her. She continued, with persistent volume, "How does that *work*?" The two friends she'd been sitting with, a man and another woman, inhaled sharply and exchanged looks. The woman grabbed her shoulder and shook it lightly. Roy and I exchanged another look.

"I am *so* sorry," Iliza's friend called to us, her eyes wide. "Iliza, you're drunk."

"Sure I'm drunk, but I still want to know—"

Looking up at Roy, I found, unexpectedly, that I just couldn't care about it. The night was too far gone. Roy was plainly furious—he had uncurled from his hunched posture in one, almost frighteningly controlled motion, his gaze fixed on

Iliza. But I was able to say to him, "Don't worry about it. Either she'll shut up and apologize, or Amy will throw her out."

On cue, I could hear Amy yelling, "Where the hell are my crutches? Oh, forget it. Iliza! Iliza. You're being a cock." I found myself laughing. "Iliza, you apologize to Asher—and Roy—right now. No, you *apologize*."

Something else happened, but I wasn't paying attention; I grabbed Roy's hand and jerked him down toward me, so he actually took a step down from his perch on the sofa arm, surprised. I kissed him full on the mouth. There was a smattering of applause, some hooting, and Amy was still yelling vengefully. I watched as Roy closed his eyes.

"Normally," I said much later to Allan, a little apologetically, "our parties are pretty tame."

He gave a dry laugh, his breath puffing out brightly against the black night air. He, Roy, and I had paused together just outside Amy's place. It was somewhere well south of 1 A.M.; we'd just said good night to Amy and Vikram after a rapid round of clean-up and many hugs from Amy.

"Asher," Allan said, "I grew up in the '70's." With deliberation, he put his hands into his pockets, a kind of punctuation.

"Okay, fine," I said, laughing, "this was *also* pretty tame. But next time I'll make sure Roy brings the coke." I nudged his side, and he rolled his eyes at me.

Allan smiled, the creases below his eyes deepening. "It's a deal. Roy—I'll see you next weekend." Roy tipped two fingers to his forehead. "Asher—"

"Good night, Allan." Impulsively, I pushed my joystick forward, and leaned to give him a hug.

He rested his hand on my shoulder for a moment after we separated. "Good night. Be well." I watched his rangy, slightly bow-legged stride as he set off down the block toward his car.

When I looked back, Roy was bouncing lightly on the balls of his feet, his head tipped up to stare at the sky. The moon had long set, and only a few stars were visible against the glare of suburban streetlights. Our cab would arrive in a few minutes.

"He looks like you," I called to Roy.

He looked at me questioningly.

I nodded up at the winter stars. "Orion. Big shoulders. Always on the move."

"Oh—hah."

"Sorry, was that too cheesy?" I rolled up to him, and he put both of his hands down to cup my face, smiling.

"I was miles away. Just d-d-didn't know what you were talking about." He bent to kiss me, darting out his tongue once.

As he broke, I exhaled. After another moment I said, "We both made it out in one piece, hm? Thanks again for putting up with all the rabble."

He smiled. "It was... interesting. I like Vik."

"Vik? Oh, Vikram. Oh, that's great to hear. Me, too. We'll have to make Amy bring him to things more." Privately I thought that Vikram seemed like he would have proposed to Amy six months ago, if he didn't think it would have scared her off. There was a kind of quiet fervor to the way that he looked at her, a low flame of feeling. I had seen it in even in the careful way that he put his hand on her lower back as they waved good-bye to us tonight. And—the spat with drunk Iliza notwithstanding—he smoothed Amy out; she seemed more centered, less frenetic when he was around.

"You looked h-h-happy tonight," Roy continued.

"Hm. I felt happy."

"Good. Good." His voice registered deeply in my chest.

"I'm glad you could see it. I know it hasn't been fun lately, not knowing... how I'll show up, any day." I reached my hand up to his. I thought about what I'd just sketched out to myself about Amy and Vikram. "I hope you know... no matter how it looks, I'm always happier when you're there."

"*Oh.*" The word was so forceful, it was almost an exhalation. I tensed with guilt at how obviously Roy had needed to hear that reassurance. My knees and arm drew in sharply; my hand twisted inward. "Yuhhh... yeah," he went on. "I was worrying about it, s-sometimes."

"I'm sorry. I'm sorry I didn't say something sooner."

He kissed me in answer. "We'll keep doing this." And I was amazed at how quickly my body relaxed again, the spasm suddenly lifting its hold.

I could hear our cab coming; the sound always seemed thinner, further off, on cold nights. As it drew nearer, we held hands, and I just looked at him, his serious brows and soft eyes, the gravity of his presence. The way the streetlights sent multiple shadows shafting off from his feet, as if he were the center of a spoked wheel.

Despite the cold, I resented the coming cab. I wanted another moment alone with him. I wanted all of them.

***

Snow was predicted for New Year's Eve, but the storm got hung up further south for a day, so it wasn't until the second day of January when Roy and I could go out in the snow.

We woke up early, just about dawn, and got ready more or less in silence, enjoying the hush of the snow densely falling past the panes, the low moan of the wind, our quiet anticipation.

As I finished bundling up in the kitchen, I could still hear Roy rummaging in my bedroom closet. When I heard a decisive *clunk*, followed by silence, I called, "Did you find it?"

"Yup." Roy emerged from the bedroom, using one hand to wheel along my folded and little-used manual wheelchair.

"Sweet, thanks."

"I'll go load it up." He disappeared out the kitchen door, letting in a brief gust of cold wind and a spray of snowflakes across the doormat. I sat, listening to the wind, my head for once peacefully empty.

When Roy reappeared, a dusting of snow already on his hair and shoulders, he followed it up with, "And now we'll load this one up—" and bent to pick me up from my powerchair.

"Hey, hey—" I laughed and threw a mock-punch at his chin. He responded by kissing my cheek as he pulled me close to his chest, one arm behind my back, the other under my knees.

I braced myself as we broke outside. The wind came against us, softly pummeling, the snow brushing across my face more like a sensation than a physical substance. As Roy carried me to the cab of his pick-up, I glanced down at the prints of his boots—there was already a good three, four inches of snow on the ground. He settled me into the passenger seat, and our eyes met as he stepped back to shut the door for me. We smiled: this was, finally, my first time riding in his truck. And who knew how many more times it might actually happen—he'd kept asking questions about wheelchair van models, since we'd first discussed it the day of the party.

Even on the road, the world was ghostly-quiet. We saw only one other car on the drive over to Crown Hill Park, going in the opposite direction. It was quickly swallowed up into the soft tunnel of snow behind us.

At the park, Roy pulled into a street parking spot at the base of the hill. Then I watched, stretching out my contracted hand, a little apprehensive, as he retrieved my tarp-covered manual chair from the pick-up bed, unwrapped it, and popped it open on the sidewalk. Again I braced myself for the cold as he opened the door, lifted me into my chair. As I settled myself in, he retrieved a blanket from the truck and wrapped it around my legs, then left me to buckle my seatbelt over it. We planned to be out for a while.

"Ready?"

"Ready."

He began pushing me, striking out into the fresh sweep of snow laid across the hill. Soon the snow would be deep enough to hide the slight depression of the paved pathways, but for now, they were just perceptible enough for us to follow, aided by our memory of the routes we'd followed over and over together that fall. Gazing ahead at the expanse of satin smoothness, the rising ghostly shapes of trees with snow blown against their trunks, the sheets and streamers of snow curling on the wind, I was startled when I heard Roy's deep voice speaking directly into my ear. I glanced back; he had bent low over my handlebars as he pushed.

"So when's the last time," he was saying, "you went out when it was really snowing?"

I had to think. "For more than a few minutes? I must have been a kid…" He knew that going out even days after snowfall could be difficult for me; I'd gotten trapped on poorly cleared sidewalks more than once, which was additionally terrifying considering that sub-freezing weather could make my power-chair's battery life drop unexpectedly.

Roy made a thoughtful noise, and kissed my cheek before withdrawing. It was getting colder; I tucked my left hand under the edge of the blanket, pulled my right arm closer to my chest.

The snowfall was growing finer, more powdery. It blew on and on, until I started to entertain a strange idea that I was watching the same snow appear, disappear, and reappear, over and over, a loop being pulled past us as Roy pushed me up the hill under a pale-grey sky. I drew up my left hand again and reached it back over my shoulder until I could briefly rest my fingertips on top of Roy's hand.

"It's all very far away," I said.

There was a pause before Roy called back over the wind, "What is?"

"That's what you said, once. You said that when I was trying to ask you about high school and the boys on the soccer team again." I turned my head until I could see him, and he nodded in understanding, or confirmation. His breath puffed out from between his parted lips, and his eyes were fixed on me.

"I'm feeling like it's all very far away right now," I continued.

Again, there was a pause before he said, "I agree." There was a slight smile on his lips.

"When we leave here—when we go back—what if the snow just stayed? For good?"

He was still smiling. "The snow will s-s-stay, but things will come back."

"And then the snow will go, too."

"Yup."

I turned my face forward into the storm again, and shouted, "Stay, snow!" I flung out my arm in a sorcerer's gesture, thinking of Prospero, though maybe King Lear would have been the better analogy. Then I had to laugh at myself.

We were almost at the columned white belvedere at the peak of the hill. It appeared through the snow in glimpses, a little temple to winter.

"Roy, stop!"

He came around to my side, looking alarmed. I was so giddy that even the momentary backsliding of my wheelchair on the slope, before Roy hastily pulled back on the handlebar, inspired only a quick flip in my stomach.

"Everything okay?"

I pulled his other hand to bring him around in front of me. This turned out to be a risky proposition: the wheel opposite his supporting hand on my chair was now rolling back down the sleep slope, sending me pivoting away from him sharply—again my stomach flipped, but I just laughed—until he quickly released his hand from mine and seized my other handlebar, bringing me up safely perpendicular to the slope.

"You're really having to do all the work here," I said, a little more seriously.

"But you're out here b-b-because I wanted to be," he said.

"That's very true and reasonable. What I like most about you, Roy, is how reasonable you are."

"Is that really what you like most about me?" He looked as if he wasn't sure whether he should be concerned or not.

"No, you're right, it's not. What I like the most about you is how I look at you or I think about you and I still can't understand how I can *feel* this much love for you. Always."

He stepped forward; he grasped my shoulders instead of the back of my wheelchair. He kissed me.

When we opened our eyes again, I didn't ask him, even though part of me still wanted to, how he imagined he could be happy with me for long; I didn't ask him if he ever maybe wanted me to just not have so many problems, so much to manage; if he ever just wanted someone who was written in the same language. I didn't say anything because I knew that sometimes, he wondered the same things about me.

We'll keep doing this.

"We'll go as far as we can go," I said.

"As far," he said.

I shouted into the wind then, "Let's *go!*" And I pointed down the slope, back down the wavering tracks we'd made on our way up, the bootprints and the slicing marks of my wheels. The tracks at the bottom of the hill had already softened, filling up with snow again.

Roy grinned in answer and swung me around; he started pushing me down the hill. At first slowly, pulling back on my chair, but then faster and faster, so that momentum was really carrying me, us, his footfalls thudding muffled behind me as he ran to keep up.

The snow beat softly against our faces, like little bursts of cold light. I leaned my face into it, shut my eyes, let it carry everything away behind me. All I could say was, *"Faster!"*

I heard his laughter, his answering shout of joy. And I trusted that at the bottom of the hill, his hands would be there to slow and steady me, to hold me safe while the storm blew away the world we'd known.

18 |

Acknowledgements

With thanks to E.J.G., K.S., L.F., J.P.C., D.G., and L.J. for their encouragement and support.

Printed in Great Britain
by Amazon

51559582R00123